DAYS

MARY ROBISON

DAYS

STORIES

Alfred A. Knopf New York 1979

This is a Borzoi Book
Published by Alfred A. Knopf, Inc.

Copyright © 1977, 1978, 1979 by Mary Robison
All rights reserved under International and Pan-American Copyright Conventions.
Published in the United States by Alfred A. Knopf, Inc., New York, and
simultaneously in Canada by Random House of Canada Limited, Toronto.
Distributed by Random House, Inc., New York.

The following stories have appeared or will appear in *The New Yorker:*
*Sisters, Doctor's Sons, Kite and Paint, May Queen, Daughters, Independence Day,
Pretty Ice, Smoke.*
Beach Traffic appeared in the January 1979 issue of *Viva.*

Library of Congress Cataloging in Publication Data
Robison, Mary.
Days.
I. Title.
PZ4.R6676Bo   [PS3568.0317]   813'.5'4   78-20607
ISBN 0-394-50444-5

Manufactured in the United States of America
First Edition

For Jim

CONTENTS

KITE

AND PAINT

It was the last day of August in Ocean City, and everybody was waiting for Hurricane Carla. Don was outside the house he shared with Charlie Nunn, poking at the roses with an umbrella. The cuffs of Don's pants were soaked with dew. His morning coughs were deep, and with each round of coughs he straightened up and clutched his cardigan to his throat.

Charlie Nunn was watching Don from an old glider on the porch. He had taken apart the morning paper, and had the sports section open on his khakis. Both men were in their sixties.

"You don't sound good," Charlie said.

"I know it," Don said. He paused in the roses and whacked at a spoke of weed with his umbrella.

A green car pulled up at the curb in front of the house. Charlie nodded at a face in the window of the car. The car door opened, and Don's former wife, Holly, got out. She was all dressed up — a pale green crocheted dress, nylons, and alligator shoes. She came up the path of flat stones that led to the house, one hand on her red straw hat.

"Come in, come in, Holly," Charlie said. He folded his newspaper and tucked it under his thigh. "Do sit down," he said.

"Thank you, no," Holly said. "I'm just here to check on my piano." She stepped onto the porch, and her hand dropped from her hat to one hip. She smiled at Charlie.

"I could kick myself for not moving it out of here long ago," she said. "Don can't play it. Unless he learned to play."

"No, he didn't," Charlie said. "But the piano's safe. I got it on top of the meat freezer, believe it or not. I built a frame for it so it won't warp if we get flooded, and it's shrouded in polyethylene."

"On a meat freezer?" Holly said. "My goodness. It's really nice of you, Charlie. Or did you even know the piano belonged to me?"

"I guess I did," Charlie said. "I used to keep track of what was whose. Last evening, I just decided everything had to be protected."

"Well, what are you going to do?" Holly said. "Are you two going anywhere for the hurricane?"

"Not that I know of," Charlie said. "I guess almost everyone else already left."

"Yes, a lot of them are staying over at the grade school," Holly said. "It's high ground." She turned and looked toward Don. "I wonder if he should be out there," she said. "What's he doing?"

"Picking mint, it looks like," Charlie Nunn said. "What can I do?"

"Nothing at all," Holly said. She tapped one of her shoes against the other.

"Let's go look at the piano," Charlie said. He got off the glider and led Holly by the wrist through the front door.

They went through the parlor and the kitchen to a small storage room at the back of the house. Charlie gestured at the piano, an upright, which was lying on one side on top of a low freezer. Inside its slatted frame, the piano was swathed in plastic wrappings.

"It looks like a coffin," Holly said. "It should be fine. It looks great. How in the world — "

"I got in some beach kids, and they gave me a hand with it," Charlie said.

"What are those?" Holly said, pointing to some flat shapes stacked in one corner.

"Sized canvases," he said. "I don't know why I'm keeping them safe. Don won't use them. He hasn't worked since he had the flu."

"He hasn't?" Holly said.

"No."

"Well," she said, "you know the only time he painted with me was when we were first married — oh, twenty years ago. Back when he was friends with some of the big names."

Charlie followed her back into the parlor.

"Oh, God, look at that," Holly said. "He left the caps off his oils. They're all clotted." She went over to Don's drawing table, in one corner of the room, and stared at the metal trays that held his paint tubes.

"I would at least like to see the canvases stay dry," Charlie said, half-sitting on an arm of the couch. "They were work."

"They predict fourteen-foot waves," Holly said.

"I heard that," he said. "If we flood out, I swear I'm taking the canvases first. I had to cut the stretchers with a miter box. They're black oak. The sizing's made with white lead from Germany and glue from Japan."

He got off the couch and went over to a closet. "Let me show you something. This makes me furious," he said over his shoulder. He knelt and eased a square of illustration board from between some storage envelopes on the closet floor.

Charlie showed Holly the illustration board. It had childish doodles of a warplane dropping a row of finned bombs, and beneath the bombs there was a pencil sketch of a pelican.

"Do you see this part?" Charlie said, circling the pelican with the tip of his index finger. "Feather perfect," he said. "It could buy us food."

"How bad is the financial situation with you two?" Holly said.

Charlie said, "I have a pension from teaching."

"You taught? I never knew that," Holly said.

"Sure. I taught shop at the junior high for twenty-three years."

"This junior high? Then you're from here?"

"Oh, yeah," Charlie said. "My dad was with the shore patrol. My mother's still alive. She lives on Decker Street. I'm told somebody already drove her to Philadelphia for the blow. One of my nieces, I think."

Don came into the parlor, carrying a handful of mint. "Aren't you scared?" he said to Holly.

"No, I'm not scared," she said. "Just exhausted is all."

"I think I'll take some of my kites down to the beach," Don said. "It's getting sort of windy already." He dropped the mint on the seat of an armchair.

"In fourteen-foot waves?" Holly said. "How smart would that be?"

Don pointed the end of his umbrella at Holly's hat. "What a thing on your head," he said.

Holly's face reddened. She said, "I'm on my way to Philadelphia, Don. I'll be at Mary Paul's." She turned to Charlie. "Maybe I'll see your mother," she said.

"Maybe you will," Charlie said, rocking forward on the soles of his shoes.

"Goodbye, Charlie," Holly said, heading for the door.

"Goodbye, Don," said Don.

"Yes, goodbye, Don," Holly said.

"I don't feel good," Charlie said, in the next hour. He and Don were in the parlor.

"Go outside and take some breaths," Don said.

Charlie frowned at the couch, which was heaped with cardboard boxes he had just brought up from the basement. He got down and lay on his back on the parlor rug. He touched his fingers to his wrist, and cocked his arm to read his pulse against his watch.

Don had changed his pants and sweater for a bathrobe and sandals. He was sitting in an armchair and drinking from a bottle of gin. On his lap was a small wheel of cheese.

"The air is so bad in here it's making me cry," he said.

Charlie had a lighted cigarette in his mouth and was smoking it while he took his pulse. Some ashes had fallen on his unshaven chin.

Don snapped the switch on an electric fan that stood on a table beside his chair. The fan wagged slowly to and fro, cutting the smoke haze over Charlie's body.

"Chess?" Don said. "A quick game while we wait?"

Charlie stubbed out the cigarette in an ashtray he had balanced on his stomach. He glared at his watch. "No, I don't want to play chess," he said. "I just want to feel better."

"You would if you ate. Only you'd better get to it, because what you see here is about all there is, and it's nearly gone," Don said. He snapped off the fan.

"You're eating that cheese with the rind still on," Charlie said.

There was a gust of wind outside, and the parlor curtains billowed against the windowsills. "You should see it out there," Don said. "From here, it looks like the sky is beige."

Charlie rubbed his stomach.

"I'll let you see what I did last night," Don said. He got up and stepped over Charlie on the way to the closet. He brought out a shopping bag and put it on the rug by Charlie's head.

"Looky here," Don said. He pulled a half-dozen kites from the bag. The kites were made of rice paper, balsawood strips, and twine, and were decorated with poster paints in bright primary colors.

"They look like flags," Charlie said.

"I made drawings of each one in a notebook beforehand," Don said. "I gave them titles. These are called 'Comet' and 'Whale.' " He showed Charlie a blue kite and a yellow one with an orange diagonal stripe.

"Yeah. What else?" Charlie said.

"This is 'Boastful,' " Don said, handing Charlie a kite. "Stay still a minute." He crossed the room with a kite in each hand.

"I'm not going anywhere," Charlie said.

Don propped the kites against the boxes on the sofa, where the light from one of the parlor windows fell on them. "These are the next to the best," he said, standing back. " 'My Beauty' and 'Moon.' "

"Right, right," Charlie said. "Let's see the best."

"This one — 'Reddish Egret,' " Don said. "It's my favorite." He held the last kite flat above Charlie's face. "See?" he said, touching a stenciled figure in the center of the kite. "It's a bird."

"Why don't you send them to Zack in the city?" Charlie said as Don took the last kite away. "He could get you some gallery space or something, I'll bet."

"I fired Zack," Don said. "It'd be fun to waste them in the blow."

"Not a chance," Charlie said.

"Why can't we?"

"I'm not getting off this floor," Charlie said, "unless it's to get in hot bathwater, and I mean up to my chin."

Don collected his kites and dropped them one by one into the shopping bag. He threw himself into the armchair and turned on the fan again.

"Holly was shocked at the mess your oils are in," Charlie said after a while.

"Oh, don't even tell me," Don said. "Holly! Her very presence is dispiriting to me."

"I don't know why you say that," Charlie said. "All she hopes for is to see you do an occasional day's work."

"I never liked to paint," Don said.

Charlie turned on his side on the floor and braced his head on his palm. "Would you turn off that fan? I can't hear myself," he said. "You liked painting when you had a model. Especially that one model."

The fan quit by itself, in mid-swing, and the noise from the refrigerator stopped.

"Uh-oh," Charlie said. "That means the hot water, too." He got off the rug and went to the window, and stood holding back the curtain. "It looks like a good one," he said. "How about flying your kites from the porch roof, if I rip up an old bedsheet? For the tails, I mean. You want to climb out there and try it?"

"I do," said Don.

C A R E

BARBARA led Leah through a coalyard to behind the elementary school. "Now look at that," Barbara said. "It's human." She pointed into the cinders at a blade of bone studded with teeth.

"That's from a cow," Leah said.

"No," Barbara said, shaking her head. The back and shoulders of her coat were soaked with dissolved snow.

"Well, I guess I ought to ask you about Jack," Leah said. She kicked a coal chip at one of the school's caged windows.

"I refuse to see him," Barbara said. "We're separated, as I'm sure you heard. We've been separated four months." She was still staring at the bone. "For a lot of good reasons. One is that I found this in his tool drawer." She opened her coat and showed a nickel-plated handgun tucked in at the waistband of her skirt.

Leah said, "Jack is the one person who shouldn't keep a revolver."

"He's so much worse since you've been gone," Barbara said. "My dad thinks it's because Jack reads so much. You know who Jack always liked, though?" Barbara leaned over and snapped one of the buckles on her galoshes. "Your sister, Bobby."

"Yes, I think he really did," Leah said. She sighed, and turned the shard of bone with the toe of her shoe. "You can tell him Bobby's wonderful. Just remarkable. She takes a lot of speed still. She's chewed a nice hole in her lip."

"Bobby's disturbed," Barbara said. "You can tell that just from the way she walks."

Leah blinked at a tiny maroon car that was circling the

playground, and Barbara said, "That's Jack, and I'm leaving." She turned up her coat collar and ran away along a narrow alley that edged the back of the schoolhouse.

"Now wait just a minute!" Leah called.

"I will not see him!" Barbara called back before she disappeared around the corner of the school's library annex.

Jack drove his car onto the playground and hit the brakes when he had pulled up beside Leah. "My wife moves pretty good whenever I'm around," he said. His face was chapped red with cold under his watch cap. He used his coat sleeve to scrape at a rust scab on the car door. "I heard you were back in town."

Leah got into the car. She said, "What have you done to Barbara?"

"My wife is just afraid of me," Jack said.

"Afraid?"

"Um-hmm," Jack said. A block away, his car began to shimmy as if it might explode. A waxed cup full of cigar butts slid off the dashboard and into Leah's lap.

Jack laughed and clicked a fingernail on the windshield, where a helicopter was wading into view.

"What do they want?" Leah yelled over the terrible beating of the machine.

The copter bobbed directly overhead, then canted off toward the lake.

"Not us," Jack said.

He bought lunch for them at a grocery cafeteria. Leah put her feet up on the seat of the vinyl booth, and watched out the bank of windows. The room smelled of warm food and of the laundered cotton blotters under the casserole trays.

Jack said, "Look at the snow flying." He nodded at the window.

But Leah saw a boy go by, pushing another boy in a shopping cart on the icy parking lot. The boy in the cart sucked cigarette smoke into his nose, and adjusted a dial on the plastic radio he was holding.

"Want to hear what I've been thinking about you?" Jack said, turning to Leah.

"Sure do," she said.

"I've decided that Europe didn't change you," Jack said, "like I hoped it would. You still want for something, as if somewhere you've been robbed."

"What have I been robbed of?" Leah said.

"Something important," Jack said. He spilled soda into his mouth. "The crux, the thrust of what — as I see it — is going on with you. And I'm talking about your whole life, not just here this afternoon." He grinned. "I mean it," he said. "What you oughtn't to be afraid of is a little more rarefied stratum, Leah. One thing I learned about being young is that there's a kind of purity of insight. You know? For example, right now I could decide to be a proletarian, a laborer, an artist, an executive." He was counting the possibilities off on his spread fingers. "But I wouldn't be you."

"I'm sorry you feel that way," Leah said. She munched ice from the rim of her water glass.

"Because," Jack said, "you're just walking it through. Just saying your lines and walking it all through. My wife is the same way."

"What way?" Leah said.

"Scared," Jack said.

"What of?"

Jack fit a piece of meat loaf into his mouth. He said, "I haven't any idea."

Jack plowed his car into a five-foot cone of dead leaves in front of Leah's father's house. Leah's father, Sweet, grinned widely and banged on the hood of his Lawn-Boy. He was driving snow off his parking spaces with a blade, and hauling a steel utility cart in which Leah's little sister, Bobby, reclined, smoking a Russian cigarette. "Park it up the street," Sweet yelled, glowing and glad for company.

Bobby pulled herself from the utility cart and came over to Jack's car. "You slept on your hair wrong," she told Leah. She threw down her cigarette. She wet her fingers and crammed a curl behind Leah's ear.

"Don't do that," Leah said.

"Jack!" Bobby said. She leaned in the car window and almost spit her chewing gum. "I just had a birthday. Guess how old I am. I'm twenty-two."

Sweet climbed down from his tractor. He yelled, "I'm going inside now for dry socks."

Leah moved Bobby and got out of the car. She brushed a ball of ash from her lap and then she walked up the snow-sopped lawn. "Wet," she said, touching the lip of the post-box. "The same color Sweet painted his station wagon."

"The same color he's painting everything," Bobby said, chewing. "Including my bicycle. Don't mess with the mail-box, Leah. Sweet'll kill you."

"But I'll tell you where the big money is," Sweet said, leading Leah into Bobby's bedroom. Sweet had been trimming baseboards and patching nail pops in the family den, and he was still dressed in working whites, his hands and face flecked with spackle. "Spraying high-rises. Just get a masking pattern cut for you, and a pump, of course, and you can go in there with a gun in each hand and your eyes closed. At fifteen hundred dollars a floor, you figure the numbers." Sweet stared at the blotter on Bobby's desk for a minute, then he picked up her wood-burning kit.

"What're you going to do with that?" Leah said.

"I don't know," Sweet said. "Make something."

They studied Bobby's closet door, where a collage of photos and cutouts was pushpinned. In one of the pictures, Bobby's boyfriend, Doug, was poking from an Army tank. There was a clipping about J. Paul Getty's grandson getting his ear sawed off. Bobby had one of Leah's sketches tacked up. It was a pen-and-ink on vellum, of a girl balanced tightrope-style on a strand of wire fencing.

Sweet squinted at the sketch and said, "A high school friend of mine knew how to draw. He's worth a hell of a lot of money now. He's a sign painter, and he raises Afghan dogs. Which made him rich. One bitch alone gives him thirty-eight pups. At three hundred fifty dollars a dog, you figure it out."

They had moved into Leah's room. Sweet leaned on his elbow, which rested between two ceramic birds on the clothes dresser. "I'm proud of this room," he said. "I tried to keep the walls nice while you were away."

Bobby came in carrying a shopping bag. She pinched off her rubber boot and emptied water from it into a terrarium that sat in a dying spray of light at the window. "Watch," she said, as a lump of slush dropped from inside the boot and spattered dirt and moss on the terrarium walls.

She sat on the end of the bed and opened the string handles of her shopping bag. "I bought a puzzle for Doug," she said. She showed a box, which was still tight in plastic wrap. "It's Niagara Falls."

Leah sat with Sweet, warming their knees before the opened gas oven. Sweet turned a wet-looking blue porcelain jug in his hands. "I think your mother wanted you to have this," he said, "after me."

"It's nice," Leah said.

"It is nice, isn't it?" Sweet said. "It's from the war."

Bobby was bent over the kitchen counter, banging the counter surface with her fist every time the coffeepot perked. She had a transistor radio plug stuffed in one ear and she was shouting a little. She said, "So a friend of Doug's offers him a hundred dollars for his motorcycle, and Doug's license is suspended for two more years anyway. Right?" She splashed coffee into a shallow cup and used it to wash down a capsule from a tin-foil wad she kept in her pocket. "But will he take it? No."

Sweet shifted his position in the folding chair and coughed through his nose. He said, "*War of the Worlds* is on tonight."

"I've seen it," Leah said. "Anyway, I'll be gone. I'm staying at my girlfriend Barbara's. Remember her?"

"The one that married Jack," Sweet said. "And didn't poor Jack get skinny? I thought he was your cousin Caroline at first."

Leah said, "Jack tells me I'm just walking through life. He says I ought to start changing."

"Could be," Sweet said. "How are you supposed to change?"

"I don't know. He wouldn't tell me," Leah said. "Incidentally, he's going back to school, he thinks. To Yale, in Connecticut."

"I know where Yale is," Sweet said.

Doug appeared at the side door holding a white sack of hamburgers and a bottle of Rock & Rye. "Remember the guy I told you about who was called Grandma?" he said to Bobby.

"The Polish guy," Bobby said. "About three and a half feet."

"That's him," Doug said. "He got blowed up when they were dropping bottom today. He flew all the way across the foundry and landed in the aluminum furnace."

Bobby crossed the room on her toes and gave Doug a kiss. "I was telling them how that guy at the Shell station is always expressing his interest in your bike."

"Forget it, Bobby," Doug said. He dumped the hamburgers out on the kitchen table. "That bike's worth fifteen hundred dollars."

"Then don't cry to me when it rusts," Bobby said.

"Listen," Doug said, putting a pickle slice on his tongue, "I'd give it away before I'd take a hundred dollars."

Around midnight, Leah saw Jack drop over the chest-high cyclone fence. He crossed the yard, and then she could hear him letting himself into the house, where she and Barbara were in bed. Leah propped herself against the headboard and tried to wake up Barbara.

"Go away," Barbara said through her pillow.

Jack opened the bedroom door and stepped into the room. His dark hair and eyelashes and his gloves and raincoat were wet, and his glasses had fogged over in the wet wind. He said, "It smells like furniture polish in here."

Leah said, "Shh. These are rich people."

"My own rich mother-in-law is lying on the floor in the next room," Jack said, "with a stack of magazines for a pillow, and a cocktail shaker still floating with ice cubes in her hand."

"What?" Leah said. "Is she kidding?"

"I forgot to ask," Jack said. He went to the glass back wall of Barbara's room. "Whitecaps," he said, "all over the lake, and the sky's full of snow." He came back beside the bed and settled into a beer-colored chair. He took out a thin green cigar and set fire to it. "I liked you better," he said, holding the burning stick match over his head and squinting at Leah, "when you had hair."

"You worry me," she said. Sleep and the cold night were in her voice. "Look at how much you're sweating."

Jack waved out the match and picked up a pair of rough wool trousers from the end of the bed. "Who does your tailoring?"

"In Italy," Leah said. She shook Barbara, who wouldn't turn over.

"Leah, what a lovely back you've got," Jack said.

She said, "You came to talk to Barbara, I think, so I'll leave."

Jack started to cry.

"Damn it," Barbara said. She got up and walked on the bed, and went naked into the bathroom. Jack threw his cigar after her. Lighted ash showered into the carpet. A drop of sweat broke on his eyebrow and ran over his chin.

"Because I believe you two should be alone," Leah said.

"Get him out!" Barbara called over the rush of shower water.

Jack pulled his fingers over his cheekbones. He said, "I can't concentrate on anything."

There was noise in the hall. Barbara's father came in. He had a big head and he was wearing dark, expensive clothing. "What is this?" he said.

Jack said to him, "Let me know when you find out."

"I wasn't here," Barbara's father said, nervously. "I've been at a GOP reception for the Governor. I was a little drunk, having a pretty good time."

He led Jack from the bedroom. Leah pulled on her wool pants and a tiny sweater of Barbara's and followed the two men to the lighted library. Barbara's mother was up, sitting in a swivel rocker. She was wearing dark glasses, holding a highball in one hand and a pink Kleenex in the other.

"Listen, Jack," Barbara's father said as he threw his body into a deep armchair. His wing tips didn't reach the parqueted floor. He drummed his fingernails on a tray that supported a thirty-cup percolator and clean china cups. "I have a lot of stuff to do. Stuff I'm going to hate like hell doing. Why don't you make some other friends? How about it? Why don't you give Barbara a little breathing space?"

"I didn't come to see Barbara," Jack said. He raised his voice to a shout: "Hey, Barbara, I didn't come to see you!"

Doug was up, laboring over his motorcycle, which he had taken apart on some newspapers on the rug in Sweet's living room. Bobby lay beside him on her stomach. She was drawing on the torn cover of the Niagara puzzle box with a flow pen. "Sweet broke the furnace again," she said to Leah. "He made it hot." She stopped drawing and spun the cardboard flap through the air like a disk toy.

Leah found Sweet watching boxers on television. He had his shoulders hunched and his elbows raised off his knees to catch blows. "Number one," he said when Leah came in. He smacked the sofa cushion for her to sit down. He pressed a tab on the TV remote control. "Look," he said, nodding at the television. In the late movie, an eye on a snaking tentacle was searching through an apartment complex. "You can have that," he said, and pointed to a tumbler of liquid on the sofa arm. "Bourbon and branch water on the rocks."

Leah got onto the sofa beside Sweet and started the drink. During the next commercial Sweet sat forward and snuffed through his nose. "After the war," he said, "I had a spray-painting job." He held his hands out as if they were pistols. "Just for weekends, way, way down, one hundred feet in the hulls of ships they were building. You were on a hairline." He pointed up and looked at the ceiling. "Hanging there."

Leah looked up, too.

"That was lead paint," Sweet said. "To stick to steel, it must be lead. You wore a respirator. But I'll tell you, most new men fell. Because the lead got them. Leave a bucket of lead paint unsealed for eight hours" — he clenched his fist — "it goes rock hard."

"Did you see men fall?" Leah said.

"I had a physical," Sweet said, "once every two weeks, and a urine analysis. Some men, after a while, couldn't even make water. Plip, plip — pure lead. But I got paid for that work. Your mother and I lived in Red Hook, on a man's front porch. She was all right then, but she was going to have a baby."

"That was me," Leah said.

Sweet bagged a foam pillow behind his neck and sat looking at the frostwork on the opened windows. Snow was sailing in, spitting on the heated TV.

"Are you going ice-fishing with me tomorrow?" he said.

"No," Leah said. She put her fingers in her bangs. "Jack's coming by. He's decided to teach me Russian."

"I wish Jack could teach Bobby and Doug regular everyday English," Sweet said. "I've been sitting here listening to them cuss all night, not believing my ears." Sweet yawned with his mouth closed and pulled with his fingers at the white hairs on his throat. "Of course, Bobby's a little girl, really. She's got plenty of time to change."

"I guess so," Leah said. She finished her drink and made a sick face. "What'd you think of what Jack said? That I need to change."

"You? Oh, you never will. You're just your mother all over again," Sweet said. "You don't know friends from enemies and you'll never be able to. When I was taking her to the hospital the last time, do you know what she said? She looked around and saw the tracks she'd made in the snow and said, 'That's good.' And I said, 'What's good?' She said, 'The tracks. They show where I've gone.' And she was right, but not only that: if you ever looked at your mother, you noticed this. You could tell everything she'd been through. You could tell it on her face. Just like yours."

"Oh, great," Leah said.

"No, it's good," her father said. "At least for your mother and you."

GRACE

B RISK Susan whips her linen from the rope," said Lawrence, as he stood at the window with his fists in the pockets of his silk robe.

"What is it?" said Grace. She sat up in bed and smoothed the green-striped sheet on her stomach.

"I was quoting Swift," Lawrence said. "I meant it's clouding up. It's going to rain."

Grace knotted the sheet at her sternum and came to the window. She squinted down on the great lawn, where Lawrence's partner, Victor Clair, was playing croquet in pointed evening shadows. Clair struck a yellow ball and lazily followed its run up a hill.

Lawrence sat in a captain's chair. He brought a cold pipe from the apron pocket of his robe. "Did you hear we bought a golf course?" he said.

"Clair told me," Grace said. "It's so nice." She sat on her heels at Lawrence's feet, her cheek against his exposed knee.

After a while, Clair knocked and came into the bedroom. A navy blazer was draped on his shoulders. He was holding the croquet mallet. "Your Melanie has our dinner ready," he said to Lawrence. "Snow peas, lamb, mint jelly."

"May I borrow your jacket?" Grace asked, looking up at Clair.

"It's not mine," Clair said.

Lawrence chuckled, and used his pipestem to scratch his white mustache.

"I took it from my brother-in-law," Clair said. "It's nothing I'd buy. It looks like Captain Kangaroo."

"Well, I'm cold," Grace said.

Clair put the mallet stick under his arm and hung the coat on Grace's back. "It's not even a nice coat," he said, sitting on the corner of the bed. "I just like wearing it because it isn't mine."

"I was talking to Grace about the golf course," Lawrence said.

"That'll be something," Clair said. He swung the mallet along the floor.

"I hope you'll name it after me," Grace said.

"Like Grace Hills, you mean?" Clair said. "Some name with Grace in it."

"That's right," she said.

"You think we're a pretty good time — don't you, Grace?" said Lawrence.

"I couldn't appreciate you more," Grace said. She dropped her sheet. "Now get going, please, so I can dress for dinner."

Grace wandered into the Italian rooms of the art museum and found John DeVier stopped before a Mary and Infant Jesus.

"It's criminal what they did there for a frame," she said, standing behind him.

DeVier turned, with raised brows. He said, "Hello, Grace. You look run over."

Grace slid up her sleeve and read her watch. "I've been up for twenty hours," she said, proudly, "playing Scrabble with my friends, drinking coffee. I feel grand."

They walked about the atrium of the gallery. Grace had a drink from a hooded water fountain.

"How are Lois and your daughter?" she asked DeVier.

"Don't mention them," he said. "They're worse for me to be around than you used to be. I've got a new car," he said. "Did I tell you? A German car, very fast. Let's go driving, you and I, and I'll watch you sleep."

"I'm not sleepy," Grace said.

"Did I tell you I have a hotel?" DeVier said. They were in his car, stopped at a crosswalk. "I only have it for a little while. Loews is taking it in July. We could see it if you'd want to. Nobody's there but the security men and a groundskeeper." DeVier's palm bumped the steering wheel and chirped the horn. A startled pedestrian in the crosswalk struggled with a grocery bag, which split and disgorged colored packages of food.

Grace said, "Tell me about your hotel. I would like to go there."

"Let's see," DeVier said. "It's on the lake, with three hundred and fifty rooms, a ballroom, a coffee bar, two restaurants and pools, three convention halls of varying sizes. It has five hundred beds, and ninety-two union-made rollaways, or had. They're all sold. Thirty thousand dollars or so worth of stoves, grills, broilers; forty-nine tons of linen, bedding, napkins, and the like, that went for — I forget what. It closed its doors on Labor Day, 1969, two million in debt."

DeVier pulled the car onto a concrete drive that led into the mouth of a parking garage. He snatched a ticket from the automatic dispenser. "Now tell me where the hell you've been the past couple years, Grace. Though I'm afraid to know," DeVier said.

"I wrote you about it," she said. "Lawrence and Victor

Clair. That's where I've been the whole time. Nowhere else." She drummed three fingers on the window crank.

"Great," DeVier said. "You and two jerks."

"You and your wife," Grace said softly.

"That's right," DeVier said.

He parked on the eighth floor and got out of the car. Grace looked at the heavily muscled triangle of his shoulders, back, and waist.

"You look very fit," she said.

"It's paradise," DeVier said, leaning back in through the driver's window. "Everything's going my way. I can bench-press two hundred pounds." He twisted the dinner ring on a finger of his left hand. "When I think of anything," he said, "I think of the beach at Cabo San Lucas, and the jungle, when I took you there. If it makes me ordinary, I apologize."

Grace shrugged and made her lower lip pout.

"The hotel keys are here in my office," DeVier said. "I'll only be a minute."

DeVier parked on the hotel's service road. He took Grace's hand and led her under a marquee with wood letters and shattered electric bulbs. They passed a pool and flaking cabanas.

At the kitchen entrance, DeVier stood on a platform and tried different keys in a slatted door.

"Let me borrow your lighter," he said in the kitchen. Grace buried her fingers in the cool lining of her purse and shuffled the contents until she brought out a butane cigarette lighter. DeVier took it to a fuse box over a deep-frying vat.

"We'll be shot if we don't find Lerner," he said, the switch prong still in his hand.

Grace followed DeVier to a dining room, where a tiered chandelier had been chain-lowered to the floor's center. A man with overlapping teeth and pitted skin was leaning on a carpenter's horse. He held a sandwich and drank from an aluminum thermos.

DeVier said, "This is Mr. Lerner, Grace."

Lerner nodded. He had a pistol holstered at his belt.

"May I have my lighter back now?" Grace asked DeVier.

DeVier patted his coat pockets. Lerner pointed his thermos and said, "Behind you," to Grace. She turned and saw a parka with a rabbit collar, empty soda bottles, and books of paper matches.

Grace grabbed a match pack and said, "Where is your telephone?"

"In the pantry," Lerner said. "Follow the cord."

Grace called Lawrence's house and got Clair. Behind his voice was music — Doris Day singing with a dance band. Clair said, "I think we miss you, Grace. I think we're very low. I've had it with playing Scrabble. Lawrence keeps making seven-letter words."

"I'm at the Clearwater Beach Hotel," she said.

"You can't be," Clair said. "It no longer exists."

"Indeed I am," Grace said.

"We'll send a cab for you," Clair said.

"Come yourselves," Grace said. "I'd like you to meet the owner, John DeVier."

"Lawrence doesn't want to meet DeVier. I know I don't," said Clair. "Is he really the owner?"

"Until July. We'll look for your car. Tell Lawrence." Grace hung up.

"Who am I going to meet?" DeVier said, behind Grace.

"You'll like them very much," she said. "Is that Lerner singing?"

"Yes, of course," DeVier said. "He's hired a combo to stay up with him in the Compass Points Room."

Grace said, "That's not Lerner. It's a radio."

"Yes, and it's a fine thing, Lerner's having a radio," De-Vier said. "Otherwise he might get bored between shifts of cardplaying and sports-betting."

DeVier led Grace back to Lerner. "Lerner's been informing me about the people who live here," DeVier said. "Apparently there are dozens. I don't care, except I might get in trouble with the health department or somebody, even though it's Lerner's job to keep them out."

"You try keeping them out," Lerner said. "I don't love this job enough for some blast-up."

"He plays cards with those who live on the lower floors, you see," DeVier said to Grace.

Grace sat and examined Lerner's battery-box flashlight. "Could I take this with me a second?" she asked.

"I guess so," Lerner said.

"Where are you off to?" DeVier said to Grace.

"I'm just going to look around. I thought I saw a shape or something when I was on the telephone."

Grace went into a lighted utility passage. She met a black man with a white wire beard, half-reclining on the tiled floor some twenty feet in.

"Where's Red at?" asked the man. He had a green pint of whiskey paused before his mouth. He motioned for Grace to sit down, and when she was seated he passed her the pint.

"Who's Red?" Grace asked. "You mean Lerner?"

"That's right," the man said. "Where's Lerner?"

"Listening to his radio," Grace said.

"Oh, yeah? Yeah? *His* radio? You don't know Frosty, do you?" the man asked.

"No, I don't think so," Grace said.

"He's confused," the black man said. "Frosty is confused. You ever been to Trinidad?"

"Are you from Trinidad?" Grace asked him.

The black man spat. He said, "Me? That's right. No, I ain't from Trinidad," he said. "Frosty is from Trinidad or someplace. I'm Ernest Robinson. I'm the day guard. Frosty and me and Lerner are the three guards."

Grace said, "Good to meet you." She took a sip of the black man's liquor. She lay close to him with her chin on her cocked palm and said, "I'm going around with this flashlight, upstairs, to see the people who live here."

"Sometimes we find some people," Robinson said. "What makes you think people live here?"

"Red told me," Grace said.

Robinson and Grace climbed the fire stairs to the third level. Robinson kicked a landing door and shone the lamp down a hall. The corridor was empty, and stank of tobacco and rug cleaner.

They moved past louvered doors to one that hung open. There a thick plug of candle wax burned in a ground-coffee tin. A dwarfish woman stepped into the orange wash of the candle's illumination. Men were asleep beneath a tarpaulin. A boy with a cloud of blond hair and a felt cap sat crosslegged in the room's center. By his knee was a pile of cigarette ends, crushed black on the rug. He stared straight into the white beam of the light.

"Don't worry," Grace said to him. "We're just checking around."

"Stay with me," the boy said. "Come in here and stay."

Robinson took her to other rooms and other floors. Grace tried to talk to a little black girl in soft blue pajamas. The girl scratched at a spot above her ankle. Her legs were folded under her, sideways, like a colt's.

On the sixth floor, a red-haired Negro in janitor's grays was laughing to himself. Robinson pointed at Grace and said, "She is here with the owner of this hotel."

"I'm pleased," said the redhead. "I'm Pierce du Croix, called 'Frosty.' "

"Do you know I used to dance here?" Lawrence said, looking up at the walls. He squared the knot of his tie, and Grace saw the discreet glint of his cufflinks. "I put people from the East up here if they weren't fit to be houseguests. In the summer, I liked it better than the Blackstone or the Palmer. That was a while ago. What kind of man would want this hotel, Victor?"

"DeVier didn't want it," Grace said. "It was given to him to dispose of."

"I wouldn't have taken it, is all," Lawrence said. "That's what lawyers are for."

DeVier met them in the lobby. Grace did not offer introductions, and DeVier said, "I understand this was quite a splendid place in the big-bands era, with film stars staying over. In one week, they say, Ginger Rogers, Frank Nitty, Mayor Daley — but he was Alderman Daley then and they put him in a room facing the avenue, not the lake."

Lawrence cleared his throat. He said, "That was before, surely. Nitty and Alderman Daley would have been before the big bands."

"You're probably right," DeVier said. "It was before I was around."

"Hell," Lawrence said, "it was before I was around. How old do you think I am?"

"Anyway," DeVier said, "I've got the register at home. Clark Gable. Louis B. Mayer. Three Presidents."

"Did they sign this register?" Clair asked. He snapped a piece of molding from a column and frowned at it.

"No, no," DeVier said. "It was like a reservation book, kept in longhand."

Lawrence moved toward a small dining room with his hands in his pockets. "Is this still called the Gold Room?" he asked.

DeVier looked confused. He said, "It's not called any-thing now. It used to be the Rose Room."

Lawrence said, "I remember the Gold Room. You ate downtown or you went hungry. One of those places where the veal tasted like the pastry and the pastry like the sole. This is pretty paneling here." Lawrence said, "What is it — cherry?" He ran his thumb along some wainscoting.

"I don't think it's cherry," DeVier said.

Lawrence pulled a radiator screen from a wall duct and hefted it. The tracery on the screen was cast to resemble a rosebush.

"Those were poured in a foundry in Skokie," DeVier said. "Commissioned for this room."

Lawrence set the ironwork down and brushed his hands together. "You've known Grace how long, DeVier?" he asked. "You couldn't have known her too long because she's not very old."

"Four years before she ever stepped foot in your house," DeVier said.

They were all in the Rose Room. DeVier had Lerner's flashlight. "Are you set to leave?" he said, turning to Grace.

"Your wife is waiting up for you?" said Lawrence.

"I am leaving my hotel, Grace," DeVier said sharply. "Locking it up. You are coming with me as planned."

Lawrence moved, and DeVier switched the flashlight on him. Lawrence covered his eyes with the shadow of his outstretched hand. "Shut it off," he said.

"It's not too funny the things you do, Grace," DeVier said. "So I thought we'd go downtown, or to Cross Point and get a room like we used to, or take a blanket up to Lincoln Park for the dawn and lie on the picnic green."

"I don't think we will," Clair said.

DeVier turned the pool of light on Clair, who squeezed one eye shut but did not hide his face. "Have you ever been with Grace?" DeVier asked him.

"Of course I have," Clair said.

"With Lawrence watching, probably," DeVier said. "Is that the way you do these things? All of you included?"

"Not that I know of," Clair said. "Larry, were you ever watching?"

"All right," Grace said. She stamped her foot. "My apologies to everyone. Or whatever is called for."

"Nothing's called for," said Lawrence.

"It's not?" DeVier said. "Then I guess it's not. Still, I feel very much like punching someone."

Clair said, "Why don't we get some food? Why don't we all do that? When we've eaten, DeVier, you can sock the maître d' repeatedly, because the owner of the only restaurant I know of that's open deserves to have his employees bashed. Then you can come up and see Lawrence's place. You owe him that, don't you? He came to your nice hotel. That sounds right, doesn't it? Doesn't it, Grace?"

"It sounds wonderful," Grace said.

SISTERS

R A Y snapped a tomato from a plant and chewed into its side. His niece, Melissa, was sitting in a swing that hung on chains from the arm of a walnut tree. She wore gauzy cotton pants and a twisted scarf across her breasts. Her hair was cropped and pleat-curled.

"Hey," said Penny, Ray's wife. She came up the grass in rubber thongs, carrying a rolled-up news magazine. "If you're weeding, Ray, I can see milkweed and thistle and a dandelion and chickweed from here. I can see sumac."

"You see good," said Ray.

"I just had the nicest call from Sister Mary Clare," Penny said. "She'll be out to visit this evening."

"Oh, boy," Ray said. He spat a seed from the end of his tongue.

"Her name's Lily," Melissa said. "She's my sister and she's your niece, and we don't have to call her Mary Clare. We can call her Lily."

Penny stood in front of Melissa, obscuring Ray's view of the girl's top half — as if Ray hadn't been seeing it all morning.

"What time is Lily coming?" Melissa asked.

"Don't tell her," Ray said to Penny. "She'll disappear."

"Give me that!" Melissa said. She grabbed Penny's magazine and swatted at her uncle.

"Do you know a Dr. Streich?" Penny said, putting a hand on Melissa's bare shoulder to settle her down. "He was a professor at your university, and there's an article in that magazine about him."

"No," Melissa said. She righted herself in the swing.

"Well, I guess you might *not* know him," Penny said. "He hasn't been at your university for years, according to the article. He's a geologist."

"I don't know him," Melissa said.

Penny pulled a thread from a seam at her hip. "He's pictured above the article," she said.

"Blessed be Mary Clare," Ray said. "Blessed be her holy name."

Penny said, "I thought we'd all go out tonight."

"You thought we'd go to the Wednesday Spaghetti Dinner at St. Anne's," Ray said, "and show Lily to Father Mulby."

Penny kneeled and brushed back some leaves on a head of white cabbage.

"I'd like to meet Father Mulby," Melissa said.

"You wouldn't," said Ray. "Frank Mulby was a penitentiary warden before he was a priest. He was a club boxer before that. Years ago."

Ray stuck the remainder of the tomato in his mouth and wiped the juice from his chin with the heel of his hand. "Ride over to the fire station with me," he said to Melissa.

"Unh-unh, I don't feel like it." She got off the board seat and patted her bottom. "I don't see what Mulby's old jobs have to do with my wanting to meet him."

"Why do you want to meet him?" Penny said. She was looking up at Melissa, shading her eyes with her hand.

"To ask him something," Melissa said. "To clear something up."

At the firehouse, two men in uniforms were playing pinochle and listening to Julie London on the radio.

"Gene. Dennis," said Ray.

"What are you here for, Ray?" Dennis said. "You aren't on today. Gene's on, I'm on, those three spades waxing the ladder truck are on." Dennis made a fan with his cards and pressed them on the tabletop.

"I'm supposed to be buying a bag of peat," Ray said. "Only I don't want to." He went around Dennis and yanked open a refrigerator. Under the egg shelf there was taped a picture of a girl in cherry-colored panty hose. "I'm avoiding something," he said. He pulled a Coca-Cola from a six-pack and shut the door. He sat down. "My niece is on the way. I'm avoiding her arrival."

"The good one?" Gene said.

"The good one's here already. I pushed her in the swing this morning until she got dizzy. This is the other one. The nun." Ray held the can off and pulled the aluminum tab.

"Don't bring her here," Gene said. "I do not need that."

"What*ever* you do," Dennis said.

"No, I wouldn't," said Ray.

"You can bring that Melissa again," Dennis said.

"I wouldn't do that, either. You all bored her." Ray drank from the can.

A short black man came up the steps, holding a chamois cloth. His shirt and pants were drenched.

"Charlie," Ray said, tucking his chin to swallow a belch. "Looking nice."

"They got me with the sprinklers," Charlie said. "They waited all morning to get me."

"Well, they'll do that," Dennis said.

"I know it," the black man said.

"Because they're bored," Ray said. He sat forward. "I ought to go set a fire and give them something to think about."

"I wish you would," Charlie said. He pulled off his shirt.

"Why the hell is he at the lead?" Melissa said. She was looking at Father Mulby, who wore an ankle cast. They were in the big basement hall at St. Anne's, and the priest was carrying a cafeteria tray. Fifty or sixty people waited in line behind him to collect plates of spaghetti and bowls of salad.

"Lookit," Ray said. "You and Sister Mary Clare find a seat and have a talk. Penny and I'll fill some trays and bring them over."

"No, no," the nun said. "It feels good to stand. I've been sitting in a car all day."

"Besides, we couldn't think of anything to tell each other," Melissa said.

"Melissa, there's a lot I want to talk about with you."

"I'm sure."

"There is," Sister said.

"Hey," Ray said to Melissa, "just go grab us a good table if you want to sit down."

"I do," Melissa said. She left her place in line and followed Father Mulby, who had limped to the front of the room and was sitting down at one of the long tables. She introduced herself and asked if she could join him.

"It's reserved," he said. "That seat's reserved for Father Phaeton. Just move over to that side, please." The priest indicated a chair across the table.

"Okay, okay," Melissa said. "When he gets here, I'll jump up." She sat down anyway. Her long hair lifted from around her throat and waved in the cool exhaust of a window fan.

Father Mulby glanced across the room and lit a Camel

over his spaghetti. "I guess I can't start until everyone's in place," he said.

"That'll be an hour," Melissa said.

"Here's Father Phaeton," Mulby said.

Melissa changed sides. Ray and Sister Mary Clare joined them and sat down, with Melissa in between. Penny came last. She looked embarrassed to be carrying two trays, one loaded with silverware, napkins, and water glasses.

Ray passed the food and utensils around. "Someone will be bringing soft drinks," he said to Melissa.

"Coffee?" she asked.

"No," Father Mulby said. "We don't serve coffee anymore. The urns and all."

"I'd like to be excommunicated," Melissa told him. "I want the thirteen candles dashed to the ground, or whatever, and I want a letter from Rome."

"I don't know," the old priest said. He forked some salad lettuce into his mouth. "If you kick your sister or push me out of this chair onto the floor, I can excommunicate you."

"What's this about, Father?" said Sister Mary Clare.

"Nothing," Ray said. "Just your sister."

Melissa leaned toward him and said, "Blah, blah, blah." She pushed her plate to one side. "I just have to hit Lily?" she asked Mulby.

"That would be plenty for me," he said.

Ray said, "Eat something, Melissa. Act your age."

"Don't mind me," she said, leaning over the table. She batted the priest's eating hand. "Is that good enough?"

"I'm afraid not," Mulby said.

Father Phaeton, a man with red hair and bad skin, asked Melissa to pass the Parmesan cheese.

"Ignore her, if you can, Father Mulby," Ray said. "I'm sure it's her blood week."

"And the saltcellar, too," Father Phaeton added.

Mulby jerked forward. His large hand closed down on Melissa's wrist. "It's not that," he said to Ray. "I can tell that about a woman by holding her hand, and it's not that."

Penny was lying on the sofa at home. She had a folded washcloth across her forehead. Her eyes were pressed shut against the pain in her head, and tears ran over her cheekbones.

"It's not necessarily a migraine," Ray told her. He had drawn a wing chair up beside the sofa. "My head's pounding, too. Could've been the food."

"I don't think church food could hurt anybody, Ray," said Penny.

The nieces were sitting cross-legged on the rug. "Why not?" Sister Mary Clare said. "It's not blessed or anything. Myself, I've been woozy ever since we ate."

"I just meant they're so clean at St. Anne's," Penny said. "And none of you are sick like I am. Don't try to convince yourselves you are."

"I'm not sick," Melissa said.

"You didn't eat a mouthful," Sister Mary Clare said. She exhaled and stood up.

"I wonder why you visit us every year, Melissa," Penny said.

"Do you mind it?" Melissa asked. "If you do — "

"She doesn't," Ray said.

"No," Penny said, "I don't mind. I just wonder if you girls could find something to do outside for a bit."

"Lily can push me in the swing," Melissa said. "Okay, Lily?"

Penny said, "You should have talked to Father Phaeton,

Melissa. They say he's dissatisfied with the life."

"That would have been the thing," Ray said. He told the nieces, "Maybe I'll go out back with you, so Penny can get better."

Penny took his hand and squeezed it.

"Maybe I won't," he said. He turned the washcloth on his wife's brow.

Sister Mary Clare stood in the moonlight by a tomato stake. She was fingering her rosary beads.

"Don't be doing that," Melissa said. She moved down to the end of the lawn, where it was bordered by a shallow stream. She bent over the water. In the moonlight, she saw a school of minnows swerve over a fold in the mud next to an old bike tire.

Sister Mary Clare followed Melissa and said, behind her, "I won't be seeing you again. I'm going into cloister."

Melissa leaned against a tall tree. She dug her thumbnail into a bead of sweet gum on the bark.

"And I'm taking a vow of silence," the nun said. "Do you think it's a bad idea?"

"I think it's a good idea, and probably what you want. I'm glad."

"If you care, I'm not very happy," Sister said.

"You were never happy," Melissa said. "The last time I saw you laughing was the day that swing broke. Remember that day?"

"Yes. Ray was in it when it went."

Melissa smiled. "He used to pay me a quarter to sit on his lap and comb his hair."

"I know," Sister said. "He still would."

Melissa hugged herself with her bare arms. "It won't matter before long. I'm getting old."

"So is Ray," Sister said. "But he's why you come here, I think."

"So what? There aren't many people I like, Lily."

"Me neither."

"Well, there you are," Melissa said. "The miracle is, I keep having such a good time. It almost seems wrong."

"You still do?"

"Every day," Melissa said, heading back for the stream. "Such a wonderful time."

WEEKDAY

GUIDRY was in bed, tangled in the oversheet. There was rain and something fresh and scented in the wind blowing across the wide floors of his second-story apartment. He was trying to get back a dream he had had, of waves as tall as palisades, which broke down into crisp white lines and lapped and overlapped on a beach.

He went stoop-shouldered into the bathroom to shave, and rested the day's first cigarette in the empty soap slot of the white sink. Someone had been in his bathroom before him. The tiles under his feet were damp. The bathtub was full of diehard suds.

"Christine?" he yelled.

Guidry found his ex-wife, Christine, on the living room couch. She had taken one of his button-down shirts from the laundry hamper and wrapped it around her hair. She had a beach towel with a Rebel-flag design looped once around her torso.

"Your door wasn't locked," she said to Guidry. Her bare legs were very long and they were skinny, with kneecaps like knobs. Her feet were long. She had thin toes.

"I made coffee," she said. "Or would you like something a little more eye-opening? There's V-8 and a bottle of vodka in my purse."

"Coffee," Guidry said.

"In a minute," Christine said. She patted a place on the sofa by her hip. "Sit down."

Guidry left and poured himself coffee in the kitchen, and then he came and stood in the center of the living room with the cup hooked in his fingers. Christine was dabbing cream on her face from a plastic pot.

"You took a bath," Guidry said.

"I had a bath. I made coffee. I'll make breakfast. Could you fix that TV?" She was looking at Guidry's Sony. Electric snow was blurring a daybreak newscast.

Guidry inhaled a mouthful of coffee and went to the TV. He screwed the tuner ring behind the channel selector.

"I don't want the sound turned up," Christine said. "Do you?"

Guidry went to the kitchen again and spilled his coffee down the sink. He got a tumbler of ice and a stalk of celery from the refrigerator.

Back in the living room, he squatted by his ex-wife's purse. It was an olive vinyl purse with a lot of snap pouches and zippers.

"Isn't Michelle supposed to be up?" Christine said.

Guidry did not answer. He poured from the quart of vodka. He put vegetable juice into his tumbler. He ruffled the red drink with the celery.

"Honey," Christine said, "do you still smoke? I need a cigarette."

"Just a minute," Guidry said.

Christine watched him gobble the drink and mix another one.

"Now," he said. "Now."

"Cigarette?" Christine said.

"Just a *minute*," Guidry said. He straightened from his crouch and rubbed the beaded glass along his cheek.

"Before you start yelling at me," Christine said, "don't you think you should put something on?"

Guidry took his drink into his bedroom. He put on beach trousers. They were baggy and made of white toweling. He brushed the hair off his forehead, using the round mirror over the wardrobe. He was thirty-one, with graying hair and a pinched-looking face. The vodka had made him drunk. He put on a blazer that had double rows of brass buttons.

Christine had positioned a tube-steel chair in the center of the living-room rug. She had made a drink for herself, and had her hair out of the shirt turban. Dark blond swirls massed around her ears and shoulders.

There was a roll of thunder outside the apartment screens, and Christine said, "Uh-oh."

"Get dressed," Guidry said. "I'm going to throw you out."

"I knew you would. I came to see my daughter."

"Michelle isn't here," Guidry said. "She's at my mother's."

"Well, I'm going. But first sit down in this chair," Christine said. She put her hands on the back of the steel chair and shook it.

Guidry sat in the chair. He felt the Rebel-flag towel being draped around his shoulders and stuffed down the collar of his blazer.

"Don't turn around," Christine said.

After a moment she came and stood in front of him. She had put on the button-down shirt, and there was an eight-inch comb in her left hand.

Guidry swallowed most of his drink. He said, "Bah." He chewed the inside of his cheek and looked at the pile of Christine's belongings that was under the television. There was a crumpled olive dress, a man's straw hat, a boxed set of records in cellophane, a French dictionary, a few paperbacks, low-heeled shoes, a cigarette holder made of yellow plastic, a copy of *L'Officiel*, and a pair of designer glasses with turquoise frames.

Christine was walking around with a pair of electric shears. She crammed the prongs of an extension cord into an outlet by the television and tested the clippers. They buzzed. In the breast pocket of the shirt she was wearing were hair scissors. She took them in her left hand and snipped them in the air.

"Tsk, tsk, they're saying. Can you hear them?" she asked Guidry.

"Are you sober?" he said. "Because if you're not."

"Relax," Christine said. She swallowed some drink and coughed. There was a tomato line on her upper lip.

Guidry squeezed his eyes shut while Christine ran the comb across his scalp. The clippers buzzed in his ears. Soft coils dropped to his lap and onto the floor.

"Oh, man," he said. "I pity you."

Christine said, "Do you? Hold still. Why do you pity me?"

"I was looking at your stuff. All the stuff you drag around with you."

"Um-huh," she said.

"You lousy big phony," Guidry said. "You're getting old, Chris. It isn't flattering anymore."

"It isn't? What isn't?"

"All that fashion stuff. Going around in towels and underpants."

She said, "What a crab you are today."

"I think you hang around with faggots," Guidry said.

"Don't forget I'm cutting your hair. You could come out of this looking pretty funny."

Guidry said, "I don't think you're taking your life seriously."

"Probably not."

"Not," Guidry said. "Just not. Your father died last year. Your daughter had her first period, which you don't even know about."

"Michelle?" Christine said.

"That's the one," Guidry said. "I had to send her up to Mom's. I know a little about it, but."

"When?" Christine said.

"A month ago."

"She's only ten."

"She's eleven."

"It's a terrible thing," Christine said. "It's the worst thing that can happen to you. I hope you don't tell *her* that, though."

"In fact, we had a party," Guidry said. "We pretended great joy. Why'd you show up with a French book? You don't speak French."

Christine held the electric razor off and handed Guidry a mirror. "It's a little bit of a shock," she said.

"Yes," Guidry said. "I'm now a seventy-year-old."

"I think it's nice," Christine said.

"No you don't."

"May I please have a cigarette?" Christine said.

"Bedroom," Guidry said. "In the shirt drawer. Do you still smoke Camels?"

"I don't smoke anymore," she said, and went out. "You look thinner," Christine said when she came back. "You look like your brother."

"Listen, I'm sorry —" Guidry began.

The front door to the apartment opened and Michelle stepped into the room.

"Hi," she said to Christine.

"Good morning," Christine said. "Do I get a kiss?"

Michelle kissed her mother and then her father. "Tell me about your life," Christine said.

"Well, Grandma's down in the car. We're going to Turnbow to the auction, and then to Indian Lake. Dad, I forgot my bathing suit."

Guidry shook off the towel and went to the apartment's second bedroom and collected Michelle's swimsuit.

"Your birthday's soon, isn't it?" Christine was saying when Guidry got back. "What would you like?"

"I don't know," Michelle said.

A car horn sounded on the street below and Michelle looked concerned.

"Get going," Guidry said to her.

"You look very nice," Christine said to Michelle as Michelle was leaving.

"I think you did a good job on his haircut," Michelle said. She shut the door quietly behind her.

"She is tall," Christine said, smiling down into the throw rug.

"She is," Guidry said. "So are you."

"How tall is she?" Christine said.

"I've no idea," Guidry said. He left the room and took a shower and dressed in his work clothes — shirt, tie, and corduroys. He went to the living room and made himself another drink. Christine was tearing the cellophane off the boxed records.

Guidry said he couldn't read the cover without his glasses.

"You couldn't anyway," Christine said. "It's French. It's sixteenth-century. It's an import." She lifted the casing on the stereo and positioned the record on the turntable. The music was lutes and violas, flutes and recorders.

Guidry pulled smoke from his cigarette into his mouth

and shot it out his nose. He said, "Well, it goes nicely with the rain."

Christine took a fat white paperback from her olive handbag. She got on the floor, her naked and narrow legs crossed among the curls she had shorn from Guidry's head. She leaned back on her hands with the book opened in her lap, and began to read aloud over the music.

"I'm sorry," Guidry said, "but stop right there."

"What?" Christine said.

"I would never read to you," he said. "I hate it."

"Oh, I see," Christine said. She reached for the cigarette Guidry was smoking. He stooped over and gave it to her.

Christine shoved herself backward along the floor until she was beside her purse. "You want me to go," she said.

"Ever since you arrived, I've wanted you to go," Guidry said. "You can clean up the bathtub first, and wash your glass. I'll sweep up the hair shavings myself."

Christine took the quart of vodka out of her bag and swigged from it. She drank with her head tipped back. Her throat worked eight or nine times. She pulled the bottle away from her mouth and lowered a purple gaze at Guidry. She was a thin-faced woman, with a great deal of last night's make-up on her eyes. She had a hook nose. "You are pretty smart," she said.

"How do you mean?"

Christine wagged her head, looking down. "Another reason I came is to tell you I'm getting remarried," she said.

Guidry said, "Hmm?"

"Yes. But it shouldn't interest you. He's homosexual. You were pretty smart." Christine began to speak quickly: "His name is Chester, which is awful, I know. And he knows. It can't be shortened to anything better, so it's just Chester and that's too bad. He is gay, and he's ugly and old. Not real old. We aren't hurting anyone. He's very funny. You would like him. I've told him all about you and he likes you anyway. We've decided to call him Uncle Chester for Michelle. He is talented. That's him playing the fiddle on this record. If you would ever talk to him, you could talk about Proust. He's practically memorized him. I don't want to talk about it. Don't tell me what you think. I will go. I am going as fast as I can gather up my things, except I'll leave the record. Please, please, don't say anything else to me until I'm gone."

Guidry took his cigarette back from Christine and turned down the music. "Well, I'm proud of you," he said. "I'm proud of us."

"I said not to talk to me," Christine said. She was bent over, loading both her arms. "I asked please."

"Look at what you did to my hair!" Guidry said. He pointed to his head.

"I know," Christine said. "You made me nervous."

APOSTASY

DONNA was late. She left the Camaro running alongside a dumpster and jogged to the all-night drugstore.

Sister Mary Divine Heart stood waiting before a back-lit wall of creams and ointments. Her eyes were bruised from lack of sleep. She wore a trenchcoat, and her hair was bound with a yellow rubber band.

Donna ticked a coin on the display window, and her sister, Sister Mary, covered her grinning mouth with a tissue and came out into the harsh light of the predawn. It was Sunday morning — a watery October. A lake breeze blew, tangling a *Plain Dealer* between Sister Mary's legs.

The women drove along the lakefront, listening to a re-broadcast of the Texaco opera on Donna's car radio. Sister Mary said wasn't it a peculiar sound track for the bait shops and sagging cottages that rolled by the windshield.

"Were you waiting very long?" Donna said, pushing in the cigarette lighter. "The reason I'm late is Mel and I had to work all night. You remember him? He's my boss. The congressman? He's done an article on prosecutorial immunity, and it's really something. It's really getting to him. It's getting to both of us."

Sister crossed her feet. She said, "I don't mind waiting. I watched *Les Girls* on the pharmacist's portable TV. Anyway, I slept plenty. I slept the whole way back on the Greyhound."

"What did they tell you in Rochester?" Donna said. She slowed the car and stared at her sister. "They said you're dying."

"Probably," the nun said. "Your last pal."

"Well, Jesus Christ," Donna said.

"Well, I'm dying," Sister said.

The road bent sharply and hugged a little industrial canal that ran by a mile of warehouses before rejoining the sliding surface of the lake.

Donna parked on the yellow grounds behind the cloister's tamed woodbine and herbarium. Sister Mary got out of the car and stood in the blotchy shade of a partly stripped plum tree, and Donna slid over to the passenger's seat.

"In a way, I envy you," Donna called through the window frame.

Sister shrugged. She scooped a bee off a spear of fern and held it under her eyes. She said, "I'm willing you my Saint Augustine."

"Goody," Donna said, and exhaled on the wings of the bee Sister was holding. The bee stung Sister, who brandished her palm with a white welt blooming for Donna to see.

Clouds hurried over the convent's grounds. On the drive adjacent to the refectory, kids were unloading pieces of a public-address system from the back of a Ford Pinto.

John Manditch was on the front porch of Donna's rental house, his hands pressed on his hips, doing deep knee bends. "Hold it a second," he said. "I might be sick." He looked down at his stomach and then he paced around in a small circle.

Donna opened the screen door and went into the house. A fat boy in a poplin blazer was sitting in the living room on top of her Utah loudspeaker. The couch had been moved. On the TV, a cheer-crazed commentator announced the morning news.

Manditch caught up with her when she stopped at a

sideboard in the hallway. He filled a tumbler with Tanqueray and used the tail of Donna's jacket to mop a puddle of gin he splashed on the tabletop.

Amy, Donna's housemate, appeared at a mirror in the hall and waxed on some lipstick. "It was my idea to have a party," Amy shouted, "but nobody will go home."

Donna went over and cupped a hand on Amy's ear. "Is there any food left?" she said.

"Who knows?" Amy said, and shook loose.

Donna stomped into the kitchen. She opened cabinets and flapped the breadbox. Proudhead was stretched out on the floor in evening clothes and fancy new shoes. He was eating fried chicken and drinking brandy.

"I have twin brothers," he said to a crouching girl. "Thirteen and eleven, with hair down to here." He pointed to his nipple with a shredded drumstick.

"Who ate the roast beef?" Donna said. She threw the refrigerator door shut.

"Some of this left," Proudhead said, pushing his paper chicken bucket toward her with a glossy dress shoe.

A young man in white slumped into the kitchen. He said, "I think I just backed over a Great Dane."

"That's our neighbor's Great Dane," Donna said. "You ran over Lola."

"I'm sorry," said the young man.

"I'm sorry," said Proudhead.

Donna squatted and sipped from Proudhead's Hennessy bottle. John Manditch walked by, holding his belly, and headed for the sink.

"John, get these people out of here," Donna said.

Manditch said, "The neighbors on all three sides have phoned the police. Thanks to you," he said to the young man in white.

"Lordy, Lordy," the young man moaned. "Why do these things happen to me?"

"Don't ever come back here," Proudhead said to him.

Donna woke up wearing a rope of cotton underpants and a madras jacket she had left over from high school. "What's that noise?" she said.

Manditch was beside her in bed, with a bottle of carbonated wine and a paperback novel. He pointed to Proudhead, who knocked a croquet ball across the hardwood floor with a hearth shovel.

"He has a nosebleed," Donna said.

"I know it," Manditch said, flattening his thumb on the bottle spout. "I told him. I forgot to shake this."

"Lift up," Donna said, trying to free her arm from under Manditch. "And who opened the windows in here? I can see my breath."

"I did," Manditch said. "We had a pipe-smoking visitor."

"We did? Who?" Donna said. "This morning?"

"About a half hour ago," Manditch said. "Want some of this?"

Donna took a drink from the wine bottle and coughed. She said, "My sister has cancer."

Proudhead sat down on a ladder-back chair and wadded a piece of white underwear against his nose.

The bedroom door came open and Amy put her head in. "I'm moving out," she said.

"Fine," Donna said. "Proudhead? Toss me my pants."

Proudhead threw the trousers. Donna pulled them on and climbed over Manditch, who had taken off his horn rims and was massaging the bridge of his nose.

Donna stood at the window. She found and lit a half-smoked Kool. She could see Congressman Mel Physell down there in the yard. He wore a clear, floor-length raincoat, and he was knocking pipe ash into a puddle of mud.

"That was going to be my zinnia garden," Donna yelled at him. Congressman Mel Physell jumped backward. He looked up and down the street. He threw his pipe into a clot of shrubs and moved away to the sidewalk, where Amy was busy loading a floor lamp into her Peugeot truck.

Proudhead and Donna were in the kitchen, leaning against the stove eating scrambled eggs from a skillet.

Congressman Mel Physell came through the side door. "Your lock's broken," he said.

"I know," Donna said. "For about two months."

She took him into the living room. John Manditch was lying on the floor carpet with his hair wrapped in a soap-smelling towel. "Aaah," John Manditch said. He unbuttoned his corduroys and revealed a full stomach.

"Who are these guys?" Mel Physell asked.

"I know them," Donna said. "Don't ask me how. I just do."

Amy walked by carrying a blow dryer and a CB radio.

"I've written some poems on prosecutorial immunity I'd like to read to you," Mel Physell said, opening a spiral-bound notebook.

"That's wonderful," Donna said. "Please do."

"I worked the whole morning on these," Mel Physell said, "though they're rough, you understand. These are just the roughs."

"That's okay," Donna said. "We'd be honored."

"Keep in mind, these are not the finished products. In fact, they're just an outline, really, a pastiche. Don't pay any attention to the first five or so. They're just scribbles and doodles, rough drafts, not worth thinking about. I just scratched them down without a nod to rhyme or meter. They're utterly worthless," Mel Physell said, and threw his notebook into the fireplace. He sat with his face in his hands.

Proudhead came from the kitchen, carrying the skillet and scraping out bits of egg with a spatula.

"Now stop being foolish," Donna told Mel Physell.

"I kag hab id," he said. He had a pen between his teeth and was searching for something in his raincoat pockets.

John Manditch got to his feet. He picked up the morning paper and sank into the sofa beside Proudhead.

Donna said, "I really want to hear the poems."

"Okay," Mel Physell said, lifting the notebook and brushing off a page. "Here we go. Don't listen to this first one. It's just a preliminary draft." He smoothed the page with his palm. "It's so wrinkled," he said, "I don't think I can read the handwriting. I can't seem to make it out. Just forget I mentioned it." He threw the notebook into the fireplace again.

John Manditch had the newspaper spread out on the coffee table. "Carborundum's striking," he told Proudhead. "Doesn't your father work there?"

"Cathcote," Proudhead said. "He works at Cathcote."

"I know Dick Burk at Cathcote," Mel Physell said.

Donna locked her teeth. "Mel," she said, "look at us."

"Three people," the congressman said, grinning. "Constituents."

Donna sighed and looked at the ceiling.

"Things are not so good," Mel said.

"Well, you've got that right," Donna said.

"They used to be good," Mel said. "Things were proper, and that's a cherished goal. Now — who knows? Now it's here come the firemen, here come the chilly-willies. You know?"

"You don't have to tell me," Donna said.

Mel Physell broke into full-throated laughter, which John Manditch and Proudhead parroted.

"You know?" the congressman said, wiping at his eyes. "Really."

DOCTOR'S
SONS

DICK was sitting at the kitchen table with his left hand resting flat, fingers spread, on a linen placemat decorated with Coast Guard flags. He was trimming his nails with a pinch clipper and crying. The mustache he had recently grown for his twenty-fifth birthday was wet with tears. He was embarrassed, and his cheeks and throat had the high color of a rash. Mrs. Sorenson, Dick's mother, sat across the kitchen table with a paperback book in her hand. She was humming along with the *Porgy and Bess* tape that was being piped from a tape deck in the family den.

Dick arched a finger and wiped away a streamer of tears from his cheekbone. He used his fork to break up the last strip of bacon on his breakfast plate. He looked out the kitchen window and said, "Here comes a pregnant girl." He clicked a fork tine on the windowpane.

Mrs. Sorenson stood up to get a better look at a pretty woman in white who was striding up the Sorensons' driveway. A fabric bag, stuffed with flyers, was slung on the woman's shoulder like a purse.

"About seven months pregnant, I would guess," Mrs. Sorenson said. "Is Spencer still out there?"

Dick nodded and shoved the window up a crack. "Here comes someone," he said to his brother, who was lying on his stomach in a nylon lounge chair on the blacktop just under the window. Spencer was wearing green swim trunks and dark glasses. His back was basted with oil. He flipped over in the chair and waved to the young pregnant woman.

Mrs. Sorenson put the window down. "I would imagine that's a volunteer who's canvassing for the school bond issue," she said.

Dick was frowning. He watched his brother chat with the girl.

"She'll be sorry she ever came by," said Mrs. Sorenson, "once Spencer gets going."

Dick sighed aloud and appeared to have difficulty swallowing. His eyes spilled tears.

"Come on, now," Mrs. Sorenson said. She opened her book.

"I'm thinking about my wife," Dick said.

Mrs. Sorenson wet her index finger with her tongue and turned a page. "Which wife?" she said.

"Gladys, of course. She's living somewhere in the Oldsmobile you and Dad gave me. I told you already."

"This sounds hard," said Mrs. Sorenson, "but we gave it to both of you."

"But she's *living* in it," Dick said.

"Don't let your father hear you complain about that. He thinks there are worse places to live than in new Oldsmobiles."

"No one but me ever liked Gladys in her whole life," Dick said.

Mrs. Sorenson sang a little with "I Loves You, Porgy." "Oh, I apologize," she said, breaking off. "You'd probably appreciate a little quiet."

"No, I enjoy the music," Dick said.

"Well, it's beginning to bother *me*," Mrs. Sorenson said. She stood and touched Dick's shirt sleeve. "I like that grille pattern," she said.

"I'd better tell Spencer to come inside," Dick said, "so that girl can get the word to the voters." He picked a navel orange from a fruit bowl and bumped it several times on the window. Spencer shifted his position on the lounge chair and grinned broadly at Dick. The pregnant woman moved off, walking backward and making goodbye gestures. When she was gone, Dr. Sorenson appeared outdoors, trailing a garden hose, and squirted the blacktop around Spencer. Steam rose from the wetted drive.

"I'm going to stop that tape," Mrs. Sorenson said, leaving the kitchen through a swinging door. Dick took his plate to the sink and cleaned it with a lilac-colored sponge.

Spencer came through the outside door, slamming the screen, and sat in Dick's chair. His chest was wet with hose water, and he had stuck a blue paper sticker over his ribs. "Thumbs Up on Issue One," the sticker said.

"That girl I was talking to," Spencer said, "her husband's on the staff at White Cross with Dad. He's a neurosurgeon."

"I'm so glad," Dick said.

"I told her she's wasting her summer campaigning for a bond issue," Spencer said. "I told her the economy's collapsing and there'll be a global depression by 1990."

Mrs. Sorenson came back into the kitchen and found Dick sniffling. She bent over and put her arm around his waist. "You're so attractive, with those blond curls framing your face," she said.

"I'm so attractive," Dick said in a squeaky voice, mimicking his mother.

"Uh-oh — Dick's in a ditch," Spencer said. "Did you see the girl I was talking to?" Spencer asked his mother. "Her husband's at White Cross with Dad."

"And I remember her from someplace else," Mrs. Sorenson said. "She's a patient of your father's. He'll be delivering that baby."

"None of us wants to think about that," Dick said.

"I told her what will happen with Eurodollars, and how the depression in 1990 will show that the 1930s depression was just one in a series," Spencer said.

Mrs. Sorenson was spraying the steel sinks with the dish rinser. "You look very tan and fit," she said to Spencer. "You seem to be having a good summer."

"I told that woman to bury her pocket change in her backyard," Spencer said. He took a pack of gum from the waistband of his swim trunks and slid a stick between his white teeth. "Come on, Dick," he said, getting up. He pulled his brother out of the kitchen by the arm.

Upstairs, in their bedroom, Spencer shoved Dick into a velours chair. "Put this on," he said, handing Dick a cordovan loafer.

Dick slid the shoe onto his bare foot. "It's too big," he said.

Kneeling in front of Dick, Spencer lifted the foot with the shoe onto his thigh. He laid a yellow scrap of soft cloth across the toe and began to shine it, buffing the leather.

"Did you just put a lot of polish on this shoe?" Dick said, shaking his foot loose. "Because look what it's doing." There was a ring of dark wax on the side of his ankle.

Spencer had his head turned. "Shhh," he said. "Listen — Mom and Dad."

There was a baritone noise from Dr. Sorenson, and Mrs. Sorenson's tinkling response.

"What are they laughing about?" Spencer said.

"I wouldn't know," said Dick. "Probably not about us."

CAMILLA

Rospo said, "Buy a nice coat for once. Buy the rabbit fur coat." They were in Hecht's — Rospo and his sister, Camilla — in the women's department. The store had just opened, but was noisy with after-Christmas shoppers returning gifts.

Camilla did turns before a mirror, modeling a cloth jacket with a waist sash.

"It's mannish," Rospo said to her in Italian.

Camilla was forty. She had been in America since her teens, though she knew English from Italy, from the Dominican nuns. Rospo was a little older. He had learned English from Camilla.

They rode to her apartment on Rospo's motorcycle. Rospo drove very fast, between lines of cars that were turning into the parking garages. Camilla balanced her shopping box on the bike saddle, between herself and Rospo. In the box was the rabbit fur coat. Camilla breathed through her mouth, and her breath streamed off sideways, like the bike's exhaust.

She lived on the ground floor of a brick row house, on Aisley Street, in Baltimore. She had never married. She lived alone. She worked nights, driving an elevator in a hotel, and she was still dressed in the elevator uniform.

"Call you up later," she told Rospo.

He left her in the alley by her house, holding the shopping box. She took the box inside, unpacked the new coat, and laid it on the bed.

At her stove, she cooked ground sausage and eggs. She carried the food to her bedroom, and ate with her elbows on her knees, the plate held in front of her, watching an early news broadcast on her color television.

When she finished with the food, Camilla cleaned her face and hands at the bathroom sink and traded her uniform tunic for the rabbit fur coat. She opened the bathroom door and stood back before its full-length mirror, smoking a Winston cigarette.

Camilla wanted the fashion model to see the coat — the fashion model who lived upstairs, the woman Anne.

The air on the steps leading to Anne's rooms smelled of new carpet and paint. Camilla pushed the door buzzer, and stepped away with a hand at her waist.

Anne opened the door. She was stooped with drink. She had charcoal make-up on her eyelids. She wore a dress that Camilla thought was made of foil.

Anne led Camilla into the living room, which had fresh paint, the color of lime, and small birch trees standing in pots. On the muslin-draped sofa sat Daniel, Anne's friend. An adding machine was on the low table before him, as well as a whiskey bottle, ice in tumblers, and a sheaf of papers. Daniel wore his glasses, and over his ears were plastic headphones. He was beating his foot as he punched the keys of the adding machine.

"He's doing taxes," Anne said. She kissed Camilla's face. "You're Rospo's sister, aren't you? I almost didn't know you, you look so pretty. You're the one who's in love with Daniel."

Camilla's face heated and she hid her chin in the collar of her coat. She tried to cover her features with spread fingers.

"He can't hear me. Don't worry," the model said. "Can

you, moron?" she said to Daniel. Daniel's head continued bobbing as he worked the adding machine. "Rospo told me about how you feel," Anne said, "when he came up once before to trim my hair. I guess he gave me a good cut. I'm not sure. We were laughing so much." Anne walked over to the record player and lifted the tone arm. "Rospo's a barber, after all, not a stylist."

Daniel looked up and smiled at Camilla. "Captain," he said, and smiled. He took off the headphones.

"She's got a pretty new coat," Anne said.

"Yes, it is new," Camilla said. "Do you like it?"

"Sure I do," Anne said.

"A great coat," Daniel said.

"I thought I would invite you to the movies, Anne. So I could have a chance to wear it," Camilla said. "To a matinee?"

Anne said, "I'd never make it through one single feature. Danny and I didn't sleep all night, you know. I was helping him do his income taxes."

"I haven't slept," Camilla said. "All right," she said after a moment. "Thank you."

"Bye-bye," Anne said, and Daniel waved at Camilla.

Camilla went back to her apartment, to her bedroom. She pushed open a window. The air that blew into the room was sharp and cold, full of the sounds of voices and cars.

She tried to sleep, but the little stand by her bed, by her pillow, seemed too close to her face. She got up and moved the nightstand. She unplugged a floor lamp and moved it back, too. She tried lying on the bed with her face toward the door to the hallway, but it was not her usual sleeping position. She lay on her back, and pulled deep breaths into her lungs. She heard a city bus with tire chains on the street outside, and the ring of a runaway hub cap.

In an hour she heard laughter, and the clack of a woman's shoes on the stairs, then a beating on her apartment door.

She left the bed. "Coming right away," she called.

She stopped to see her living room on the way to the door, and it was clean except for an open jar of apple butter that was stuck with a bread knife. She put the jar on a window ledge, behind a metal blind.

The fashion model kissed her own index finger and touched it to Camilla's nose. "You look like we woke you up," she said. "We are done with this man's taxes."

Daniel winked at Camilla. He said, "I spread a rumor that you have a piano down here."

"We want to use the piano," Anne said. "You'll let us, won't you?" They came into the living room, holding hands. "This is a nice place. You didn't tell me it was so nice, Danny."

Daniel said, "Sure. Captain's got a nice place. She has amber bulbs in her lamps." He was carrying the whiskey bottle by its neck with his free hand. He gave the bottle to Anne, who gave it to Camilla.

Anne threw off her high-heeled shoes and climbed onto Camilla's couch. Camilla laughed, watching the fashion model shake her shoulders and flat belly.

Daniel sat on the bench before the piano. He exercised his fingers like a concert musician.

"Oh, I see," Anne said after a while. "You can't play the piano. You don't know how."

Camilla drank a lot of the whiskey, very fast.

"Showing off?" Anne said. She took back the bottle and

had some swallows. The low gray light from the window
washed over her cloud of hair and the silver dress. Her
mouth was open and she crooned.

Camilla got the bottle and drank more. "Be careful of my
floorboards," she said, seeing the fashion model's bare feet.
"Rospo sanded off my varnish. You'll have splinters."

Anne said, "What else did you buy, besides the coat?"

"This is the first time I've seen you out of your elevator
uniform," Daniel said. "Including the time I took you to
Keppler's for clam chowder. Me for chowder, rather. I
think you preferred the navy bean."

Anne said, "Try on whatever else you bought."

"This coat is all I bought to wear," Camilla said. "I
bought a magazine."

"Try something on," Anne said. She blew hair from her
nose. "Let's see you in your other clothes. Model them for
us."

"All right, I will, I guess," Camilla said. She went into her
bedroom and closed the door. She removed her uniform
trousers, pulling them off by the cuffs. She stood before the
closet, barelegged in socks and underpants. She took a white
blouse and flannel skirt from the closet hangers and laid
them on the bed. She put more clothes on the bed — Jamaica
shorts, a black sweater, cotton pajamas. She dressed at last
in the black sweater and a pair of leather chaps.

"Those are Rospo's," Anne said when she looked at the
chaps. "He wears them when he rides his motorcycle. I've
seen him in them."

"I don't dress so as to be noticed," Camilla said. "I'm not
as pretty as you. Where's Daniel?"

"He went up to my place and conked out, probably,"
Anne said. "He left his bottle for you, though, since you

were having such a good time with it. Wasn't that nice?"

"Did you tell him anything?" Camilla said. She made noise sitting down in the leather pants.

"Of course not," Anne said. "He was just being nice. He is nice. He buys me everything new. My whole apartment." She put her head on the sofa arm and looked dreamily at Camilla. She said, "It's so lucky for me."

Camilla's phone rang from the bedroom and she moved to answer it. "Hello, hello," she said, hoping it was Daniel.

"What's up?" Rospo said. "You sound happy."

"No. I'm low. I feel like I can't get a breath today," Camilla said. "I must have emphysema." She stood in the bedroom doorway, holding the phone receiver, and watched as Anne slid off the couch and began to crawl on all fours. "Daniel was here before and left," Camilla said in Italian.

"With Anne? What'd they say about your apartment? What I did with the wallpaper."

"Watch out for your knees," Camilla said to Anne.

"I'll make it," Anne said.

Camilla told Rospo in Italian: "Your whore from up-stairs is going to cough up whiskey all over the floor you have never varnished."

"Drunk?" Rospo said. "It's eleven o'clock in the morning."

"Thank you for coming," Camilla said to Anne. "Come again and stay."

"I'm so sick," Anne said. She had reached the door. "See you later." She crawled through.

"I could kill you," Camilla said into the phone when Anne was gone. She sat on the bed that was strewn with her clothes. "You repeated to Anne every word I said about Daniel."

"That was a mistake," Rospo said. "They're very happy, you know. You don't have a chance with Daniel."

"Thank you," Camilla said. "But sometimes things can change. Nothing's permanent."

"No, it was a mistake," Rospo said. "Those two are just alike and they're very different from you. They are like me."

"Okay, then," Camilla said.

"They're not like you."

"Okay, Rospo," she said.

"At least Anne's nice about your interest. Did she see your new coat?"

"Yes. I think it depressed her," Camilla said.

WIDOWER

I'm up now," Nicky said, before our dad came in. Nicky was still under the bedcovers, his hair twisting around his smallish face from under his Phillies cap.

I was already at the window. We lived near the Atlantic then, in a wooden one-story. I was trying to read the sky.

"It's nine-thirty, lazy bums," Dad said. "I can never get you stirring, Beth, without this." He gave me a half cup of coffee.

Dad was a dentist, a big bald man with powdery hands and a pinched mouth full of gold-crowned teeth. "I can never get Nicky stirring at all," he said.

We looked at my ten-year-old brother. He was barely sitting, held up by his arms, staring at his collection of beach shells.

"He does seem to need help," I said.

Dad ran a finger along the seam at the back of Nicky's overturned starfish.

"Five more minutes, please," Nicky said. He turned back the bedclothes. He was wearing orange underpants with white piping. We both had burns from rubber-rafting in the surf the day before. Our eyebrows were bleached, and so was the down on my thighs. My skin felt crisp and too tight.

Dad left and I took the mug of coffee from the dresser top and drank. Nicky put on canvas shoes and a yellow polo shirt.

"Here he comes again," I said to Nicky. Dad came back and stood outside the door, whistling, and jiggling the coins in his pockets.

"Yep, I hear her coming up the drive," he said. "Her car tires spattering the gravel — "

"He can*not*," I said to Nicky. "It couldn't be later than nine o'clock. She isn't due yet."

"Who isn't?" Nicky said.

I said, "Mrs. Clark." Mrs. Clark was one of Dad's girlfriends.

Nicky groaned and he cut his throat with his pointer finger. I leaned into the hall.

Dad was swiping at the shaving soap on the backs of his jaws. "It's Nicky that worries me," he said. "He isn't wearing trousers."

"I'm waiting for you to stop hectoring me," Nicky said.

I drained my coffee cup and Dad handed me a stub of paper, a grocery tab. On the back, in pointy scrawl, was a list. "Things to talk about," he said, "if the conversation gets stalled."

"It won't," I said, reading the list. " 'Books, tackle and bait, beach moves.' What does 'beach moves' mean?"

"Just how every year the sand gets pushed around and the landscape is different here," Dad said. "The same conversation you had with Nicky at dinner last night."

Nicky said, "Beth, what do *you* think is the best tackle for marlin?"

"All right, all right," Dad said, retreating down the hall.

"If the damned beach would quit moving around, I might be able to opine," I said.

"All right," Dad called.

Nicky got out of bed and came across the room and performed what I thought was a startling and eerily correct impersonation of Katharine Hepburn. He said, "Oh, kiss me, Stewart." He pulled off his baseball cap and drew a forearm across his brow as he had seen pitchers do on television. He spat something from the end of his tongue.

"For you," Dad said. He had come back, with a tumbler of citrus juice, which he held out to Nicky.

"Thank you, no," Nicky said. "Give it to Beth or drink it yourself. I think you put mashed-up aspirin in it for my sunburn, which doesn't hurt."

"Your loss," Dad said, and gulped the juice.

When Dad and Nicky were gone, I got into my swimsuit, and then I put a sundress with patch pockets over it, and stepped into rubber beach thongs.

Dad was leaning against the mantel in the living room. He had the *Inquirer* quartered and was studying the editorial page. Nicky was in the swivel rocker, eating dry cereal from a Sugar Pops box.

"This is something," Dad said. He looked up from the paper. I knew he wanted to tell about what he was reading.

"What do we do with Mrs. Clark?" I said. "Is she a swimmer?"

Some of Dad's girlfriends refused to go to the beach. They were in their fifties mostly, like Dad, and didn't want to be seen in bathing suits.

"Swims better than you do," Dad said. "Roller skates better, too."

"I'd like to see that," Nicky said. He snapped a cereal bit in the air and dropped it into his upturned mouth.

My father coughed through his nose. "She's a good swimmer, though," he said. "I hope you'll give her a break. Hell, I've been up since six o'clock this morning. I've got everything ready — the awnings up, the outdoor shower fixed. I raked down the lawn. Do you hear me?"

"We're listening," I said.

Nicky said, "Didn't I meet Mrs. Clark at the Star Market?"

"She liked you very much," Dad said. "But she hasn't met Beth here. You two are alike in a lot of ways, Beth."

I sat down on the sofa, which was bristly on the backs of my burned legs. I was radiating heat. I noticed Nicky squinting at me.

"They are alike in ways," Nicky said, and went back to crunching cereal.

"What's her first name?" I said.

Nicky said, "Hammerhead. Hammerhead Clark." He laughed until the veins were standing out on his neck.

"Okay," Dad said to him.

"Helen Highwater," Nicky said.

"Her name *is* Helen," Dad said.

I went to the kitchen to poach an egg and toast a slice of bread. I poured my morning teaspoon of Maalox and swallowed it. I was fifteen years old and I had an ulcer that was just beginning to heal. I could hear Nicky still laughing in the rocker.

Dad came in. "What's going on?" he said. He put a fingernail beside a tooth and cleared away a thread of orange pulp.

"Just Nicky," I said.

"A real nitwit," my father said. "Here's something I found last night in a box in the attic, under the awning poles." He handed me a Kodak snapshot of Mom. Mom held a tissue in the photo and was wearing her hair in a French twist. "She was crying in that picture," Dad said, "but you can't tell it. That was in Springfield. She'd been hacking up onions for a stew."

"I don't remember," I said.

Dad said, "You weren't here yet."

Nicky joined us, wearing my pair of red-framed sun-glasses under the bill of his baseball cap. He made drum noises with the spittle in his mouth while our father talked to us about Mrs. Clark. Dad called Mrs. Clark Helen.

"I was a patient a long time before I was a dentist," he said. "I know a little about suffering. Okay, Nicky, cut it out."

Nicky had imaginary pliers in both his fists and was yank-ing and wrenching at one of his own back molars and whimpering with pain. He did this whenever Dad men-tioned being a dentist.

"Helen's suffered a little and her loss was more recent than ours. She's still a bit tender." He lifted his head and the several chins under his jaw smoothed. "I know I go on too much with you two. You're my only audience."

"That's a big lie," I said. "You blab to everyone you get in your chair."

"They don't listen," Dad said.

I ate at the kitchen table, trying to chew each forkful eighteen times. Still, I got up from the table with a fierce point ignited just above my navel. I marked on the back of my hand the time for taking my stomach tranquilizer, and then I stood at the sink and rinsed the dishes. I got out the vacuum cleaner.

Dad was in my way as I tried to sweep. He was restacking magazines, adjusting furniture. He spent a long time lining up the rolled bottoms of the bamboo shades on the screened front porch.

I was pushing the sweeper back into its utility closet when I was sprinkled with cold water. Nicky was back in the rocker, absently squeezing little lines from his squirt gun.

"Better stow that," I said.

"Beth," Nicky said, very seriously.

"Nicky," I said.

"Don't you hurt?" he said. We compared sunburns. His stomach was nearly tomato-colored. My chest and my nose were bad.

"Eleven o'clock," Dad said. "Time for Helen." He came across the living room and into the short hall that led to the bedrooms. He went into his room and shut the door.

"It's Helen time," I said to Nicky.

Helen was a shock-haired woman with dimples that bracketed her lipsticked mouth when she smiled. She wore owlish glasses, and she was tanned a rich mud color. She had swimmer's legs. She smelled of peppermint, and she was chewing gum. "Let's sit on the porch," she said. "By all means."

"Dad's making himself beautiful, Helen," I said. "Do you want a drink of something?"

I fixed vegetable juice cocktails while Helen talked to Nicky on the front porch.

"Solarcaine," Nicky was saying when I joined them again. Nicky was shivering all over. He hugged himself.

"The only thing that works is a tea bath," Helen said. "It takes the sting out of a burn."

"Dad said it would wreck the tub," Nicky said.

Helen said, "Piffle."

I sat with my elbows on my knees and my dress drawn up off my hot legs.

"Your father thinks I'm a reader," Helen said. "He thinks I read all the time and I never do. It's an impression I never bothered to correct."

"I won't tell him," I said.

"Tell me what?" Dad said. He had changed his clothes and was stepping onto the porch. He wore a white collarless shirt I had never seen and bright blue trousers. Five or six dark spots appeared on the belly of the shirt, and I twisted to see Nicky, but Nicky had his arms folded.

"Who squirted me?" Dad said.

"That's for making me wait, Doc," Helen said. She had Nicky's water pistol.

"Don't tell me it wasn't worth the wait," Dad said. He turned his thick body to model his shirt. On the back of the shirt, in several bright colors of thread, were embroidered Mexican flowers and leaves.

The phone rang and Dad said, "Beth."

I answered in the kitchen.

"Dr. Maurice?" a man's voice said.

"Who's calling?"

"Well, I'm here at the shore for a week," the man told me, "and last night at dinner I broke off three-quarters of a tooth on a bone in a pork chop — a big piece of filling. It hurts. The pain is really devastating." The man laughed a little. "I need to see someone and, I guess, have an extraction."

I explained that Dad was on vacation, and that he only worked Thursdays and then out of the office of Dr. Eisenstein.

"I know. I called Eisenstein, and his wife said he was in New York and that if it was an emergency I could try Dr. Maurice. I think it's an emergency. When I close my eyes I see red."

Dad came up behind me, scowling, and took the phone from my hand. I went back to the porch, where Nicky was telling Helen about a movie we had seen on the boardwalk.

"He's just waiting on top of the mesa," Nicky said.

"The first guy or the second guy?" Helen said. She seemed to be interested.

"Is this the Clint Eastwood?" I asked.

"Yes," Nicky said. "Clint Eastwood is just waiting on top of the mesa for the second guy." He told Helen most of the movie, and only when it was winding up did Helen start to look out the screen at our yard and at the big wooden tourist home across the street.

From the kitchen, I heard Dad saying, "You're telling me a sad story, but I don't even have my technician today. You should go to the mainland. I see. Well, without X-rays ... Why? Why do pregnant women see OBs instead of GPs?"

Helen said, "Beth, do you know I've got an ulcer, too?"

"Right now?" I said.

"I'll always have it," she said. "But right now it's stopped hurting and I eat just what I please."

I said, "Do you know what really helps me?"

"Swimming in the ocean," Nicky said in singsong.

"Swimming really seems to help," I said.

"I know," Helen said. "Because it relaxes you. I'm dying to go swimming."

"Me and you both," Nicky said.

"Well, let's do go. Doc can find us," Helen said.

I went for the towels and beach tags and the straw tote full of sun stuff while Nicky began nervously telling Helen about a film we had seen on the late show the weekend before. It was an old comedy, and Nicky had memorized the funniest lines.

Before he had got very far, Helen said, "I'm way ahead of you, Nick. That's one of my all-time favorites."

"Yeah? Well, do you remember . . ." Nicky said and told her about the movie anyway.

PRETTY

ICE

I WAS UP the whole night before my fiancé was due to arrive from the East — drinking coffee, restless and pacing, my ears ringing. When the television signed off, I sat down with a packet of the month's bills and figured amounts on a lined tally sheet in my checkbook. Under the spray of a high-intensity lamp, my left hand moved rapidly over the touch tablets of my calculator.

Will, my fiancé, was coming from Boston on the six-fifty train — the dawn train, the only train that still stopped in the small Ohio city where I lived. At six-fifteen I was still at my accounts; I was getting some pleasure from transcribing the squarish green figures that appeared in the window of my calculator. "Schwab Dental Clinic," I printed in a raveled backhand. "Thirty-eight and 50/100."

A car horn interrupted me. I looked over my desktop and out the living-room window of my rented house. The saplings in my little yard were encased in ice. There had been snow all week, and then an ice storm. In the glimmering driveway in front of my garage, my mother was peering out of her car. I got up and turned off my lamp and capped my ivory Mont Blanc pen. I found a coat in the semidark in the hall, and wound a knitted muffler at my throat. Crossing the living room, I looked away from the big pine mirror; I didn't want to see how my face and hair looked after a night of accounting.

My yard was a frozen pond, and I was careful on the walkway. My mother hit her horn again. Frozen slush came through the toe of one of my chukka boots, and I stopped on the path and frowned at her. I could see her breath rolling away in clouds from the cranked-down window of her Mazda. I have never owned a car nor learned to drive, but I had a low opinion of my mother's compact. My father and I used to enjoy big cars, with tops that came down. We were both tall and we wanted what he called "stretch room." My father had been dead for fourteen years, but I resented my mother's buying a car in which he would not have fitted.

"Now what's wrong? Are you coming?" my mother said.

"Nothing's wrong except that my shoes are opening around the soles," I said. "I just paid a lot of money for them."

I got in on the passenger side. The car smelled of wet wool and Mother's hair spray. Someone had done her hair with a minty-white rinse, and the hair was held in place by a zebra-striped headband.

"I think you're getting a flat," I said. "That retread you bought for the left front is going."

She backed the car out of the drive, using the rear-view mirror. "I finally got a boy I can trust, at the Exxon station," she said. "He says that tire will last until hot weather."

Out on the street, she accelerated too quickly and the rear of the car swung left. The tires whined for an instant on the old snow and then caught. We were knocked back in our seats a little, and an empty Kleenex box slipped off the dash and onto the floor carpet.

"This is going to be something," my mother said. "Will sure picked an awful day to come."

My mother had never met him. My courtship with Will

had all happened in Boston. I was getting my doctorate there, in musicology. Will was involved with his research at Boston U., and with teaching botany to undergraduates.

"You're sure he'll be at the station?" my mother said. "Can the trains go in this weather? I don't see how they do."

"I talked to him on the phone yesterday. He's coming."

"How did he sound?" my mother said.

To my annoyance, she began to hum to herself.

I said, "He's had rotten news about his work. Terrible, in fact."

"Explain his work to me again," she said.

"He's a plant taxonomist."

"Yes?" my mother said. "What does that mean?"

"It means he doesn't have a lot of money," I said. "He studies grasses. He said on the phone he's been turned down for a research grant that would have meant a great deal to us. Apparently the work he's been doing for the past seven or so years is irrelevant or outmoded. I guess 'superficial' is what he told me."

"I won't mention it to him, then," my mother said.

We came to the expressway. Mother steered the car through some small windblown snow dunes and down the entrance ramp. She followed two yellow salt trucks with winking blue beacons that were moving side by side down the center and right-hand lanes.

"I think losing the grant means we should postpone the wedding," I said. "I want Will to have his bearings before I step into his life for good."

"Don't wait too much longer, though," my mother said.

After a couple of miles, she swung off the expressway. We went past some tall high-tension towers with connecting cables that looked like staff lines on a sheet of music. We were in the decaying neighborhood near the tracks. "Now I know this is right," Mother said. "There's our old sign."

The sign was a tall billboard, black and white, that advertised my father's dance studio. The studio had been closed for years and the building it had been in was gone. The sign showed a man in a tuxedo waltzing with a woman in an evening gown. I was always sure it was a waltz. The dancers were nearly two stories high, and the weather had bleached them into phantoms. The lettering — the name of the studio, my father's name — had disappeared.

"They've changed everything," my mother said, peering about. "Can this be the station?"

We went up a little drive that wound past a cindery lot full of flatbed trucks and that ended up at the smudgy brownstone depot.

"Is that your Will?" Mother said.

Will was on the station platform, leaning against a baggage truck. He had a duffle bag between his shoes and a plastic cup of coffee in his mittened hand. He seemed to have put on weight, girlishly, through the hips, and his face looked thicker to me, from temple to temple. His gold-rimmed spectacles looked too small.

My mother stopped in an empty cab lane, and I got out and called to Will. It wasn't far from the platform to the car, and Will's pack wasn't a large one, but he seemed to be winded when he got to me. I let him kiss me, and then he stepped back and blew a cold breath and drank from the coffee cup, with his eyes on my face.

Mother was pretending to be busy with something in her handbag, not paying attention to me and Will.

"I look awful," I said.

"No, no, but I probably do," Will said. "No sleep, and I'm fat. So this is your town?"

He tossed the coffee cup at an oil drum and glanced around at the cold train yards and low buildings. A brass foundry was throwing a yellowish column of smoke over a line of Canadian Pacific boxcars.

I said, "The problem is you're looking at the wrong side of the tracks."

A wind whipped Will's lank hair across his face. "Does your mom smoke?" he said. "I ran out in the middle of the night on the train, and the club car was closed. Eight hours across Pennsylvania without a cigarette."

The car horn sounded as my mother climbed from behind the wheel. "That was an accident," she said, because I was frowning at her. "Hello. Are you Will?" She came around the car and stood on tiptoes and kissed him. "You picked a miserable day to come visit us."

She was using her young-girl voice, and I was embarrassed for her. "He needs a cigarette," I said.

Will got into the back of the car and I sat beside my mother again. After we started up, Mother said, "Why doesn't Will stay at my place, in your old room, Belle? I'm all alone there, with plenty of space to kick around in."

"We'll be able to get him a good motel," I said quickly, before Will could answer. "Let's try that Ramada, over near the new elementary school." It was odd, after he had come all the way from Cambridge, but I didn't want him in my old room, in the house where I had been a child. "I'd put you at my place," I said, "but there's mountains of tax stuff all over."

"You've been busy," he said.

"Yes," I said. I sat sidewise, looking at each of them in

turn. Will had some blackish spots around his mouth —
ballpoint ink, maybe. I wished he had freshened up and put
on a better shirt before leaving the train.

"It's up to you two, then," my mother said.

I could tell she was disappointed in Will. I don't know
what she expected. I was thirty-one when I met him. I had
probably dated fewer men in my life than she had gone out
with in a single year at her sorority. She had always been
successful with men.

"William was my late husband's name," my mother said.
"Did Belle ever tell you?"

"No," Will said. He was smoking one of Mother's cigarettes.

"I always liked the name," she said. "Did you know we
ran a dance studio?"

I groaned.

"Oh, let me brag if I want to," my mother said. "He was
such a handsome man."

It was true. They were both handsome — mannequins, a
pair of dolls who had spent half their lives in evening
clothes. But my father had looked old in the end, in a business in which you had to stay young. He had trouble with
his eyes, which were bruised-looking and watery, and he
had to wear glasses with thick lenses.

I said, "It was in the dance studio that my father ended
his life, you know. In the ballroom."

"You told me," Will said, at the same instant my mother
said, "Don't talk about it."

My father killed himself with a service revolver. We never
found out where he had bought it, or when. He was found
in his warm-up clothes — a pullover sweater and pleated
pants. He was wearing his tap shoes, and he had a short

towel folded around his neck. He had aimed the gun barrel
down his mouth, so the bullet would not shatter the wall of
mirrors behind him. I was twenty then — old enough to find
out how he did it.

My mother had made a wrong turn and we were on But-
tles Avenue. "Go there," I said, pointing down a street beside Garfield Park. We passed a group of paper boys who
were riding bikes with saddlebags. They were going slow,
because of the ice.

"Are you very discouraged, Will?" my mother said. "Belle
tells me you're having a run of bad luck."

"You could say so," Will said. "A little rough water."

"I'm sorry," Mother said. "What seems to be the trouble?"

Will said, "Well, this will be oversimplifying, but essen-
tially what I do is take a weed and evaluate its structure and
growth and habitat, and so forth."

"What's wrong with that?" my mother said.

"Nothing. But it isn't enough."

"I get it," my mother said uncertainly.

I had taken a mirror and a comb from my handbag and I
was trying for a clean center-part in my hair. I was thinking
about finishing my bill paying.

Will said, "What do you want to do after I check in,
Belle? What about breakfast?"

"I've got to go home for a while and clean up that tax
jazz, or I'll never rest," I said. "I'll just show up at your
motel later. If we ever find it."

"That'll be fine," Will said.

Mother said, "I'd offer to serve you two dinner tonight,

but I think you'll want to leave me out of it. I know how your father and I felt after he went away sometimes. Which way do I turn here?"

We had stopped at an intersection near the iron gates of the park. Behind the gates there was a frozen pond, where a single early-morning skater was skating backward, expertly crossing his blades.

I couldn't drive a car but, like my father, I have always enjoyed maps and atlases. During automobile trips, I liked comparing distances on maps. I liked the words *latitude*, *cartography*, *meridian*. It was extremely annoying to me that Mother had gotten us turned around and lost in our own city, and I was angry with Will all of a sudden, for wasting seven years on something superficial.

"What about up that way?" Will said to my mother, pointing to the left. "There's some traffic up by that light, at least."

I leaned forward in my seat and started combing my hair all over again.

"There's no hurry," my mother said.

"How do you mean?" I asked her.

"To get William to the motel," she said. "I know everybody complains, but I think an ice storm is a beautiful thing. Let's enjoy it."

She waved her cigarette at the windshield. The sun had burned through and was gleaming in the branches of all the maples and buckeye trees in the park. "It's twinkling like a stage set," Mother said.

"It is pretty," I said.

Will said, "It'll make a bad-looking spring. A lot of shrubs get damaged and turn brown, and the trees don't blossom right."

For once I agreed with my mother. Everything was quiet and holding still. Everything was in place, the way it was supposed to be. I put my comb away and smiled back at Will — because I knew it was for the last time.

DAUGHTERS

Now we can talk," Dell said to her daughter, Charlotte. "If you've still got your bus fare. You didn't lose it, did you?"

They had just run out of the rain and into a concrete bus shelter, which had a long wooden bench. Dell sat down on the bench and pulled Charlotte down beside her. Charlotte was eight — too old to be held on a lap. The rain was falling and blowing in overlapping sheets, and Dell and Charlotte were both soaked.

"Be still," Dell said. She jerked her head back to avoid the spokes of a toy umbrella that Charlotte was twirling. They were in downtown Erie, in Perry Square, and the sky over the office buildings across the park from them was low and bruise-colored. Charlotte got down from the bench and went to the street curb, with the umbrella trailing behind her.

"Come back here and talk to me," Dell said. "I won't ask you again. Get out of the rain."

"I've still got it," Charlotte said. She stepped back under the roof of the shelter and uncurled her fingers to show a wet quarter. Her damp hair fell onto her shoulders, and her ears were exposed.

"I found a snake," she said, pointing at the gutter.

Dell got up and went to the curb with Charlotte and held her umbrella above them. They were bending over, watching an earthworm coiled next to the river of water in the gutter, when a new Mercury station wagon pulled into the near lane. Dell straightened up and squinted at the car's headlights. A Buick swerved to get around the station wagon, and its horn blew.

A man in a black raincoat got out of the passenger side of the station wagon. "We know," he said to the Buick. He opened a newspaper over his head, and ran over to where Dell and Charlotte were standing. "We *thought* it was you," he said, and tried to catch both of them under the spread of his newspaper. He was about forty, with dark hair.

"You remember Pierce, don't you?" Dell said to her daughter.

Charlotte nodded at the man in the raincoat.

"We're in a bit of a hurry," the man said.

Dell said, "You two should just go on, Pierce. Nicholas is going to get rammed from behind, the way he's blocking traffic."

Nicholas was behind the wheel of the station wagon. His hand came up and he pressed his palm on the windshield in greeting. He was wearing an old wide-brimmed felt hat.

"Pierce, you really should go on," Dell said. "The bus will be along any second."

"I meant for you to hurry up and get in the car," Pierce said. "Come on. We'll take you wherever you're going."

"We're going to my father's house. We couldn't think of riding in your car. We're wet to the skin." Dell turned to Charlotte, who had the earthworm draped over her index finger. "Put that worm back," she said.

More horns blew.

"Come on, Charlotte," Pierce said. He threw his newspaper into the street and grabbed the back of the little girl's neck. Nicholas leaned over and opened the back door for her. Dell collapsed the toy umbrella and followed her daughter inside.

"Hello, Nicholas, and how are you?" Dell said.

"I'm fine," Nicholas said, looking at Dell in the rear-view mirror. He was white-haired, and about ten years older than

Pierce. The two men were owners of a greenhouse and garden center, and they lived together in a townhouse on the south side of the city. Dell and Charlotte had rented their third floor for a few months after Dell divorced her husband. Charlotte was small then, and just learning to stand.

"We're *both* fine," Pierce said, shouting a little over the whack of the windshield wipers. "We're moving books. Hey, look at you."

"I'm sorry," Dell said. She tried to fluff up the scalloped wet curls around her face. "This is a new car, isn't it? I can smell the upholstery, and we're wringing wet."

"And now you've ruined it," Pierce said. "We'll have to get an even newer one. Won't we, Charlotte?"

"So much room!" Dell said.

"It's a barge and a headache," Nicholas said, steering the station wagon into the heavy afternoon traffic that ran around the square. A truck horn sounded behind them.

"Pay no attention," Pierce said.

Dell wiped beads of rain from her handbag. She said, "Could I possibly get a dry cigarette from someone?"

"Lean up, Nicholas," Pierce said. Nicholas turned sideways behind the wheel, and Pierce fished a pack of cigarettes from his raincoat pocket. "There," he said. He flipped the cigarettes over the seat to Dell. "That thing by your arm is an ashtray if you pull it out."

"Thank you," Dell said. She snapped a paper match and looked at it cross-eyed as she lit her cigarette. "We've been swimming all afternoon at the YW, is why we're downtown. I'm taking a lifesaving course, and Charlotte's in Polliwogs."

"You're lucky to have your days free," Pierce said. "We're moving these books from the office at the plant store to the house, and we had more than we knew. Mostly gardening stuff. This is our third trip, and we're about out of boxes."

Dell said, "Would it be all right if Charlotte sits in one of the boxes? Because she already is."

"Be our guest," Pierce said.

Charlotte had found an empty carton in the well behind the back seat. She was sitting in the box, with only her head showing. "Pierce," she said, "do you still have Django?"

"In fact, Charlotte, we don't," Pierce said. "Django ran away."

"Did he really?" Dell said.

Pierce shook his head. "Hit by a car," he mouthed.

"I'm so sorry," Dell said in a low voice.

"Where'd he go?" Charlotte said. She was using her finger to draw in the steam on the back window.

"College," Pierce said. "He went to get his bachelor's."

Charlotte ducked her head and shoulders into the box.

"Your daughter's turning shy," Pierce said to Dell.

"She's turning into a petty thief," Dell said.

Nicholas took a quick look at Dell in the mirror. "Really?" he said. "Is she any good?"

"I guess so. I hadn't thought of it in those terms," Dell said. She unbuttoned the side pouch of her handbag and brought out a packet of dollar bills.

"It's grand larceny, not petty theft, if she took that," Pierce said.

"This is just *one* thing she took," Dell said, riffling the bills like playing cards. "Seventy-four dollars. It was in the pocket of her jumper. She says she found it on the golf course. You know the golf course next to my father's place? Did I tell you we're living with my father right now?"

"She probably did find it, then," Pierce said. "Golfers are wealthy."

Dell said, "The trouble with this much money is I can't spend it and I don't know who to give it back to."

Nicholas stopped the car for a red light. Pierce reached over and twisted a knob, halting the windshield wipers. "I think we're out of the rain," he said.

The car started with a jolt, and Dell said, "Nicholas, I don't believe I've ever ridden with you. Pierce was always the driver."

"He only just got his license," Pierce said. "It's tricky, driving in the wet."

"Do I turn here?" Nicholas said. A diesel truck blew its air horn behind them. "I guess I don't."

"He's a little embarrassed," Pierce said, "just starting to drive at his age. He's never liked being told how to do anything."

"Yes, you do want to turn here, to get to my father's place," Dell said.

"I had my signaler on," Nicholas said.

Pierce said, "We'll let you alone, Nicholas. We know we're in safe hands. But you do have to merge if you want to get onto the parkway."

"We *are* merging," Nicholas said.

Dell directed Nicholas down several suburban streets, then past a new shopping mall and onto a road that went uphill parallel to a golf course. "There we are," she said. "The fourth house. The drive starts behind those hedges."

The rainstorm hadn't reached South Shore Drive, but some of its clouds still streaked the late-afternoon sun that was streaming over the broad lawns and slate roofs of the houses. In a neighbor's yard, a man in yellow coveralls rolled a silent mower toward a three-door garage. Nicholas drove the Mercury up the driveway.

"This is very, very nice," Pierce said. "Is this where you live, Charlotte?" He pointed to a thicket of plum trees and then to a trim line of dogwood saplings. "Good planting there," he said.

Nicholas stopped the car on the concrete turnaround in front of the low red-brick house.

"There's my father," Dell said. She touched a fingernail to the car window. "He must have just got home from the office."

Dell's father, Gene, was smiling at them from under one of the linen shades at a window in the living room. One of his hands came up by his ear and he wiggled his fingers.

"Let me kiss you," Dell said to Pierce and Nicholas. "I might not see you again for a while."

"Hold off on that," Pierce said.

Gene came out of the front door of the house. He was wearing gray flannels and a red cardigan sweater and a pair of slippers, which slapped against the driveway. He opened the tailgate for Charlotte, who jumped out and landed on the concrete drive on all fours. Gene picked her up and twirled her over his head, turning her small trunk in his hands. "You're a bad Charlotte," Gene said. "Say it."

"I am bad!" Charlotte said, gasping and laughing.

Gene brought her down and released her. "What's up, Nicholas?" he said. "Come on inside. I've got gin gimlets."

"We hadn't seen your gardening," Pierce said. "We are impressed."

"That's thanks to the soil," Gene said. "Use a little lime

and you could even grow tobacco here. Nicholas, now I know you want a drink, don't you?"

"You have no idea," Pierce said, getting out of the station wagon. "He's just been through a trial."

"Oh, yeah?" Gene said.

"People were driving like crazy idiots," Dell said.

"Let's do have a drink," Pierce said to Nicholas.

Nicholas stayed behind the wheel. "First of all, Pierce, I'm in no mood for a drink," he said. "You shouldn't be either, at five o'clock. We were going to the race track tonight, remember? Plus I'd like to get the books finished, if nobody minds." He looked straight ahead as he spoke.

"Will you calm down?" Pierce said. "We have time for one drink." He came around to help Dell out of the car.

"Well, I'm going to take the boxes home," Nicholas said. "I'll unpack them myself and then I'm going to the track. Do you have the money, Pierce?"

"You have money," Pierce said. "Drive carefully."

Dell said, "Stay in touch, Nicholas. Give us a call in the very near future."

Nicholas nodded and backed the car out of the drive.

Charlotte had run into the open garage at the end of the driveway, and was throwing old toys out of a box there. The three adults walked up the lawn to a flagstone patio, which was set about with wrought-iron furniture.

"I refuse to baby-sit for Charlotte tonight," Gene said to Dell, "so you can't go anywhere. For once, I want to be in my bed and sleeping by ten o'clock."

"You will be," Dell said. "I'll get Charlotte to bed on time myself, if I have to force her."

"I mean it," Gene said. He led Pierce and Dell into the foyer, and hung Pierce's raincoat behind a louvered door.

They entered the wide, deep living room. The table lamps were already lit, and their silk and parchment shades were glowing orange. A brass light with an emerald shade stood on top of the piano. There was a full ice bucket on a side table behind the couch, and Gene mixed gimlets and shook them up in a tall silver shaker.

"I'm interested in you and Nicholas," he said to Pierce. "I want some trees for inside here. For this room. I was thinking of little laurels." He filled a glass and handed it to Pierce. "You two have a nursery someplace, don't you?"

"We can get you a tree at cost," Pierce said. "But we're generally wary about putting hearty trees indoors. They get restless."

"I've seen them thriving," Gene said. He swallowed half of his drink and refilled the glass from the shaker. "Dell," he said, "get your daughter in here. Everybody come over here and sit down around the coffee table. This is a meeting. Charlotte!"

Dell went out and reappeared with Charlotte, who was holding a plastic doll with blond hair. They found seats around the low mahogany table. Gene had the cocktail shaker in front of him.

"This is about you," Gene said to Charlotte. He took an old-fashioned jeweler's watchcase out of his sweater pocket and tipped back the hinged lid with his thumb.

"Oh," Charlotte said. She got down from her seat beside her mother and sat on the floor.

"You know what's in this box, don't you, Charlotte?" Gene said.

"I broke his watch," Charlotte said.

"First she stole it, then she broke it," Gene said. He held up a gold wristwatch with a shattered crystal. The hands of the watch were smashed against the watch face. "This was my anniversary present," Gene said. "Your mother gave it to me, Dell, on our twenty-fifth."

"Charlotte, this is terrible," Dell said. "Look at that watch. I feel so sorry for Grandpa."

"I feel sorry for him," Charlotte said. She tugged with her fingers at the carpet.

Dell said, "It was an important, special thing of his."

"It was irreplaceable," Gene said.

"All right, we're sorry, Father," Dell said. "But I don't think this is the time for a reprimand."

"Reprimand?" Gene said. "Hell, I just want to know why she did it."

"You're on the hot seat," Pierce said to Charlotte.

Charlotte looked at him out of the corner of her eye. She rocked forward and planted her spread hands on the carpet. She tried to do a headstand.

"Getting upside down won't help," Pierce said.

Dell picked a cigarette from a lacquered box on the table. She said, "Charlotte, go get Mommy's lighter from the bedroom."

"You send a kid for a cigarette lighter?" Gene said. He gestured to Charlotte to stay where she was.

"Probably unwise," Pierce said.

"I do it all the time," Dell said. "It never occurred to me."

"Well, when you come home and your home is a charred black hole, it will occur to you," Gene said.

"I just wanted to shoo her off, Father," Dell said, putting down the cigarette. "I've wanted to discuss this stealing thing with her, but not now. She's embarrassed and on the spot. Aren't you, Charlotte?" She leaned over and looked at her daughter. "Are you crying? Do I see tears?"

"No," Charlotte said. She was lying on her hip.

"Neither do I," Gene said. "Frankly, Charlotte, I could wring your neck."

Dell said, "Thank you very much, Father. Now I think it's time for Charlotte and me to take a bath."

"I wouldn't know what time it is," Gene said. "I don't have a watch."

Dell refilled her glass and tasted her drink. "My, these are strong," she said. "Excuse me, Pierce." She took the cocktail and Charlotte and left the room.

Dell balanced her drink on the side of the tub in Charlotte's bathroom and turned on the tub faucets. Charlotte came into the room on tiptoes.

"A bath, and then I'm tucking you in," Dell said.

"Now?" Charlotte said. "It's so early. I don't even see the moon."

"What I see is you," Dell said. "And unless I'm mistaken, you have completely disrobed. Hop in."

"I'm so hungry," Charlotte said.

"Didn't I offer you dinner downtown? Would you eat it? No, you wouldn't."

Dell left Charlotte in the bathroom. A few minutes later, she came back carrying a tray with a dish of sliced fruit and cheese and a glass of pink soda on it. She put the tray down on the closed toilet seat. Charlotte was in the tub, surrounded by a flotilla of bath toys. Dell undressed, dropping her clothes on the bathroom floor. She retrieved her gimlet and stepped into the tub behind her daughter.

Charlotte twisted around and sniffed. "God," she said, "why are you drinking that?"

"Don't say 'God' to me, Charlotte," Dell said. "You are

in enough trouble. Your grandfather's had it with you, in case you don't know. You walked off with Dr. Hanley's paperweight. Then you brought home Trish Bydecker's doll buggy. You stole seventy-four dollars from somebody. Now you've crushed Grandpa's poor watch. Think about it."

"I'm sorry," Charlotte said.

Dell finished her drink and submerged her glass in the bathwater. "You've got one last chance, Charlotte," she said. "I think you'll agree it's better for us if you stay out of sight and under the blankets tonight. Do I hear a 'yes'?"

Charlotte heaved a sigh and nodded.

Dell's face was flushed. She said, "So you see, if you go to sleep in a while, or even pretend to go to sleep, I'll buy you a car tomorrow."

"What kind of car?" Charlotte said.

"Like Pierce and Nicholas's. You can drive around town and get some new friends."

"What will you really buy me?" Charlotte said.

"It depends," Dell said. "Stretch Armstrong?"

Charlotte made a little shiver of pleasure. "Would you really?"

"Really," Dell said. "Sleep tonight, and Stretch Armstrong when you wake up." She soaped Charlotte's back and drew numerals on it with her fingernail.

When Dell came back to the living room, she was wearing a silk blouse, pleated trousers, and patent leather slip-ons. She found her father pacing up and down with a library book open in his hand. He had his reading glasses on. Pierce was sitting on the couch, holding a golf putter. He looked a little stunned. Some of his dark hair had come forward on his forehead.

Gene said, "Sit down, Dell. I want you to hear this. 'It seemed as though I had left my body and was about ten yards above myself, floating in the air,' " he read. " 'I could see myself down below, crushed beneath the car's tires, but I felt no pain. I was strangely detached. I wasn't even interested.' "

"Don't let Father read to you," Dell said to Pierce. "You poor thing."

"I'm all right," Pierce said. "I'm about ten yards above myself, feeling no pain or even interest."

"This proves life after death, I think," Gene said.

"What about dinner?" Dell said. "Have you offered Pierce dinner, or were you going to put him in a coma first?"

"I'm hungry, too," Gene said, "but let me finish. I was reading about this guy who was hit by a car." He closed the book. "I'll just tell you, all right? The guy is legally dead. Heart stopped. No brain waves. You know what he hears?"

"How can he hear anything?" Pierce said.

"Angels," Gene said. "A choir thing starts up for him."

Pierce had poked the golf club into his shirt sleeve and worked it up to his shoulder, so that his left arm stuck straight out. "I wouldn't hear choirs," he said. "I hate choirs."

"It's different at my age," Gene said.

"I think I have to leave now," Pierce said. "Gene's liquor has punched me between the antlers."

"Gets you, doesn't it?" Gene said.

"Come on in the kitchen with me, Pierce," Dell said. "I'll phone for a cab, and you can watch me fix dinner."

"There are some strip steaks thawing in the icebox," Gene said.

Pierce shook his arm, and the golf putter fell down his sleeve and onto the carpet.

"Everyone must have a clear conception of his or her relationship with God," Gene said. He spoke with great precision, pronouncing each syllable.

"I don't," Pierce said. He followed Dell into the kitchen.

She called a cab on a wall phone in the breakfast nook, and then she walked back and forth under the cabinets, gathering plates and shaking out napkins. She took a head of lettuce from the refrigerator and began washing the leaves under cold water at the sink.

Pierce had found a bone-handled carving knife and sharpener, and he drew the blade back and forth against the rod. "We haven't taken in another boarder since you," he said. "You left quite a hole in our lives, Delilah, which I could manage to live with if you'd phone once in a while."

"I haven't called because of guilt," Dell said. "I know I still owe you that rent money. You've been very nice not to mention it."

"Oh, for heaven's sake," Pierce said.

"No, I do owe it, and I'm working on paying you. You'll get a pleasant surprise in the mail someday."

"Don't embarrass me," Pierce said. He put the knife down and picked up his gimlet glass from the top of the dishwasher. "Don't put a strain on our friendship."

"I know how angry I made Nicholas," Dell said.

"Nicholas is an old lady," Pierce said. "Anyway, he and I are thinking of getting a divorce. We've been at each other's throat twenty-four hours a day lately. You hang on to your money. You got a rough break from your husband, and you need all the money you have. Nicholas and I don't need it, and you know I'm telling the truth, because I'm generally such a bitch about finances."

Dell twisted a knob on the stove and then looked out the

bay window in the breakfast nook. A pair of headlights was moving down the drive. "I see your cab, Pierce," she said.

Pierce went out of the kitchen, and when he came back he was stuffing his arms into his raincoat sleeves. "Gene conked out," he said. "He's using the afterlife book for a pillow." Pierce stooped a little and squinted out the bay window. "Why, that's Nicholas. What do you know? He came back for me."

"Will he come in?" Dell said.

"He's too ashamed," Pierce said. "He'll sit out there in the car until I go to him." He leaned forward and kissed Dell on the mouth.

Charlotte came into the kitchen wearing a clean nightgown. She had a sheet of red construction paper with a crayon drawing of a dog on it.

"Is that Django?" Pierce said. "For me?"

"Yes, I drew it for you," Charlotte said. She looked at her mother.

"Instead of being asleep," Dell said.

There was a quick, loud horn blast from the driveway. Pierce shrugged and worked the collar of his raincoat into place. "I'm being called," he said.

RELATIONS

I saw my cousin Junior three times in San Francisco before we spoke to each other. Twice I saw him at the Southern Pacific Depot, at the cafeteria there. Once I saw him walking in the opposite direction on Post Street. The time we did speak, Junior was sitting on a curb in front of Curl's Bar, wearing a ponyskin jacket, chain-smoking, letting the rain cool his cup of coffee.

Actually, now that I think about it, it may have been in Chicago, at the Harvey restaurant in the train station, that we first spoke. Junior came in carrying a string-handled Marshall Field sack of tape reels. It was raining. I can say that. A winter rain, with a wind that bent up the spokes of my umbrella. Whatever year it was, I remember Max Roach was playing with Miles Davis still. John Huston was filming *The African Queen*.

Definitely it was San Francisco, because my boyfriend, Warren, was off at Great Lakes, going to Korea then, and I told Junior how broken up I was. Junior said he was upset, too, only it was over a girl who had chopped off her hair and gone down to San Diego to work in a marine hardware foundry. Right, and Junior had his *carton* of tape reels pushed under the window awning at Curl's, to keep it out of the rain. They were radio tapes, I think he told me, made at Voice of America, where he had a job as a technician, or a sound engineer.

So we were talking, and Junior kept complimenting my Shetland Islands sweater, which was new and waterproofed with oil, so that it smelled like a fuel tanker. He wanted me to give him the sweater, and I finally agreed to trade it for his ponyskin jacket. His voice was trembling, I remember. He said he had had a headache ever since Lent. He never gave my sweater back. But then, he never saw his leather jacket again, either.

He took me to his apartment — and now I'm sure it was in California, because I remember it was a ten-room apartment on Shattuck that I had thought of renting. His mother, my Aunt Barbara, was visiting, or living there. She was hunched over a sinkful of dishes, wearing yellow rubber gloves.

She went on and on about my father — how sad my father got after I left home. Junior was sharing the cigarette Aunt Barbara had balanced on a soap dish, and he tried to stick up for me in his own way. He said I had never cared a damn whether my parents were happy or sad, and that I wasn't supposed to, or Aunt Barbara said I wasn't supposed to.

Anyway, there was a man there, in a checkered suit and felt hat. He wore the hat inside the house and he was drinking bourbon. Junior introduced the man as Brad something, a builder. I don't know if he was Junior's friend or Aunt Barbara's.

Junior and I wandered around the back rooms of the apartment and I opened some doors and said I envied the closet space. Junior had his glasses off, massaging the bridge of his nose, and said he'd rather think in mathematics, in calculus, than in English. He said sometimes, on drugs, he thought in camera slides, and sometimes, sometimes in wallpaper patterns.

He played horn music for me on a tape recorder in a portable valise. I sat at a roll-top desk by a bay window. Junior crushed up Dexedrine cartwheels and poured the powder into his coffee. Then he balanced himself on the steam radiator. He had a rice-paper scroll tacked up that ran the length of the wall. I think I fell asleep on my elbow for a minute. When I came to, Junior was still on the radiator, talking about bamboo-brush painting. After a while he got hiccups and came down and sat on his heels and held his breath. I pounded him on the back between the shoulder blades and cured his hiccups, or maybe they went away naturally, but anyway, we left then. Junior drove me to my flat on Divisadero. He drove me on a motorcycle that was strapped with saddlebags full of tapes from Voice of America, which I don't believe I ever got a chance to hear.

He kissed me between the eyes. He said he'd visit me again when I stopped being embarrassed.

Years later we met in the Fillmore district. I spotted Junior as he stepped out of a taxi, and mopped his brow on my sweater, which he was still wearing.

The builder, Brad, the one who was Junior's or Aunt Barbara's friend, was driving the taxi. He was dressed in the same suit as that night on Shattuck Avenue, but his hair had gone gray, and he wore dark glasses. He was moving around on the front seat of the cab, cleaning the window with a lady's white glove. He urged me to get in, or Junior urged me, and we rode over to a basement room Junior said was his office.

Junior's office had blackboards, graph sheets pinned up, ashtrays as big as fish bowls. He scribbled on the blackboards with pink chalk, and got mad when I asked what his business was.

But the next summer I got a phone call I'm almost sure was from Junior. I had a standing floor fan going in my room, so I could barely understand, but I think Junior said anyone interested in credentials could phone Berkeley.

It was later, when I was *working* in a Harvey restaurant, in Chicago, that Junior telephoned from O'Hare and said he needed a ride. He was in town for the Democratic convention, he said, and he said that his headache was worse.

It took a long time to get to the airport and then I had trouble parking. Junior was waiting for me at the American Airlines baggage ramp. He wore a beige turtleneck and had a bouquet of mums.

He talked about having children. He asked if I didn't think having children was a fine idea. He said usually he enjoyed hearing my opinions, or else he said he had *never* heard my opinions and wondered if I had any.

We were in my Plymouth, on the expressway, passing a red weedfield that was going to be subdivided into a housing tract, when Junior asked to be let out. I pulled onto the berm and stopped. A bad wind was throwing paper trash and Dixie cups around.

Junior said he was going to walk back and sit on a pine bench he had seen. He said after that he might run around in the weedfield until he got lost, and maybe he did, too, because I only saw him one other time before I saw him dead at his funeral — he was hit by a post office truck in a Florida crosswalk on his way to Disney World — and that one other time I saw him was when Aunt Barbara got married to a man who owned a soda-bottling company.

BEACH

TRAFFIC

VIRGINIA drank coffee. She leaned against the cosmetics counter in the family store, and watched her daughter, Cheryl, turn a wire carrousel that was hung with lipsticks on cards.

Cheryl, a thirty-year-old in a sand-colored dress, had her hair wound on a dozen metal curlers and covered with a plaid scarf.

"Sonny's coming," Cheryl said. She selected a brown eyebrow pencil in a silver tube.

"I hope he doesn't want Vern to help him caulk his boat," Virginia said. She went to the doorway at the front of the store, where she could see her husband, Vern, deep in the yard between their store and their house. Vern was planing a board that was C-clamped to carpenter's horses. A round sucker popped out his right cheek. The paper stick stuck from his mouth like a cigarette.

"Your father is making a picnic table," Virginia said to Cheryl.

"That makes five tables, and he's yet to sell one this year," Cheryl said. "Besides, summer's over. Maybe Sonny can talk him out of it. May I have this?" Cheryl asked. She held up the pencil.

"Yes," Virginia said, "but no one can talk to Vern about his tables." She went out the doorway and walked beneath a line of tall cottonwoods that fronted the two-lane highway.

The road was clear of beach traffic, though it had once been the main route to Atlantic City. Five unfinished picnic tables were set on the wide gravel shoulder of the road. There was a sandwich board, opened on legs, on which Virginia had painted: "$66.00."

"Good day," Virginia said.

"Good day," Vern said, dragging a piece of sandpaper across his board. He stopped sanding, and stared at his work shoe, then squatted and tied the lace. Unfiltered cigarettes fell from his breast pocket into the grass.

"I haven't seen you today," Virginia said. "I didn't hear you get in bed last night, and I don't believe I heard you getting up this morning."

"You were having a time," Vern said. He crushed the lollipop with his teeth and extracted the stick from his mouth and put it into his trouser pocket.

"What was I doing?" Virginia said.

"Thrashing," Vern said. "I thought your teeth might be hurting you again." He picked a curl of wood shaving off his shoulder. "Or you were having a nightmare."

"Yes, I was dreaming," Virginia said. "I dreamed of a truck that could go into the sea and bring out fish."

A salt-stained Buick pulled into the store's parking lot. An old couple got out and helped each other along the walk.

Virginia followed the couple into the store, and showed them where to find laundry soap and a tin of aspirin.

"Watch the curves if you're going north," she said, punching the keys on the cash register. "People are in such a rush."

After the couple left, Virginia sat on the soft-drink refrigerator. Behind her was a bright wall of unguents and sun sprays.

A man with a helmet came in and walked toward the magazine rack. He wore tight vinyl chaps over his dungarees. *Triumph* was silkscreened on the back of his jersey.

The man had a cigarette while he looked at magazines. Virginia got off the refrigerator and went behind the register. She stood in front of a display of photographs she had taken. She'd cut mounts from illustration board and framed the pictures with aluminum and glass. One photo showed Vern riding alone on a Ferris wheel. Another picture was of Cheryl at the shore. The photograph was cropped to an extreme close-up, and overdeveloped, so that Cheryl's eyes and mouth looked black and torn.

"Cousin?" the motorcyclist said.

"May I help you?" Virginia said.

"What are those?" the man said, nodding at Virginia's photographs.

"Nothing."

"You sell many of those?"

"No," Virginia said, "because they aren't for sale."

"Why are they there, then?" the man said. "Did you shoot them?"

Virginia began to take the pictures down, stacking the frames against her breasts.

"Don't do that," he said. "I like them."

"Were you going to buy something?" Virginia said.

Cheryl reappeared in the doorway. She had painted her eyes, and brushed her hair into thick waves.

"Hello, cousin," the man said to Cheryl.

"Sonny still isn't here," Cheryl said.

"Who is Sonny?" the motorcyclist asked.

"My former husband," Cheryl said. "He's very big."

"Well, he'd have to be," the motorcyclist said. He went to Cheryl and put his arm on her shoulder. "Do you like being this tall?" he asked her. He turned Cheryl around toward the lot so she could see the large motorcycle tilted on its kickstand. "Want to go for a ride?" he said.

"I saw it," Cheryl said. "Of course not. I'm waiting for Sonny."

"And if she weren't, her father would have yard work for her to do," Virginia said.

The motorcyclist took his arm off Cheryl and lit another cigarette.

Sonny's car, towing a boat trailer and with the amplified radio at full volume, turned into the parking lot. On Sonny's trailer was a fiberglass catamaran, and on the roof of his car a twenty-foot mast was fixed with cable. Orange safety pennants licked the wind at both ends of the mast. A radio voice from inside the car sang, *"Your mamma won't mind, your mamma won't mind."*

"Looks like Sonny's got a catamaran," the motorcyclist said to Cheryl.

Sonny came into the store. His cheeks were burned and he was wearing wraparound glasses. He grinned at Virginia, and shook his fingers on Cheryl's head, mussing her hair.

"Is that your bike?" Sonny asked the motorcyclist.

"Well," the man said, "I did all the work on it myself."

"What happened to your photographs?" Sonny asked Virginia.

"I got tired of them," Virginia said.

Sonny tilted open the lid on the floor refrigerator and pulled out a bottle of soda. "So, what have you been doing?" he said to Cheryl.

"I'm hurt you didn't take me sailing this morning, Sonny," she said.

"I had to take someone I owed a favor to. She was not a good sailor."

"Is that right?" the motorcyclist said, blowing a plume of smoke toward the ceiling. "She was not a good sailor?"

"What's going on?" Vern said from the doorway. He was holding a spanner wrench.

Sonny said, "Vern, you look well. I see you have your picnic tables all lined up by the road. And how about that new one you're working on? What'll it go for?"

"A lot of money," Vern said. "It's redwood."

"Everybody likes your tables, Vern," Sonny said. "But they don't fit on cars."

"Same old argument," Vern said. He pointed his wrench at the motorcyclist's stomach. He said, "Who is this, Sonny? A friend of yours?"

"A customer," Sonny said. "He got the word on your tables. He'll take six."

"I was leaving," the motorcyclist said. He put on his helmet, and crushed his cigarette against the floor with his boot toe. "I might come back," he said to Cheryl and Virginia.

"Please don't," Sonny said. "You're too ugly."

"Aren't I ugly?" the motorcyclist said, snapping his chin strap.

Virginia put cold ham and paper plates of cream salad on one of Vern's tables in the backyard. Sonny made a pitcher of mint tea. He told about sailing and about television shows he'd seen. He talked about the city — how dangerous the city was.

"I'm amazed you've lasted this long," Cheryl said. "Working in an office."

"Don't start an old fight, Cheryl," Sonny said.

"I've learned how to strike back," Cheryl said, grinning. She shot her fists in the air in combinations and, from a low crouch, drove a whipping left into Sonny's thigh muscle.

Vern said he was going to put some apple chunks out for the squirrels. "And if you want some color in your pictures," he said to Virginia, "get your camera. You can catch some jays swooping in."

When Vern left, Sonny said, "He seems recovered."

"Oh, he's weak, but he doesn't complain, Sonny," Virginia said.

Cheryl said, "For a while after, his words were slushy."

Out on the highway, a siren whooped and they listened to it fade.

"That's an ambulance, not the patrol," Virginia said.

"It's probably that motorcyclist," Sonny said.

Virginia sat at the picnic table awhile with her legs crossed and her arms folded. Sonny and Cheryl went to the middle of the lawn, out of the shade, and spread Sonny's boat sails to dry.

"I'm going in for a sweater," Virginia called to them.

In the house, in the bedroom, she lifted a large yellow box from the top of a dresser. In the box was a twin-lens camera and a light meter.

Virginia was taking a small can of film from the refrigerator when Vern came in.

He said, "You going to use that, Ginny? I'll tell the kids."

"Don't tell them," Virginia said. "I was just thinking about it."

"Better get a picture," Vern said, with his hands on his hips. "Everyone looking so nice."

They walked back to the lawn. Virginia began to take light readings with the meter.

"Get ready for pictures," Vern said to Sonny.

Vern licked his palms and smoothed back his hair. He twirled up the points of an imaginary mustache.

"What's the occasion?" Sonny said, taking off his glasses.

"Just a good day," Vern said, "whenever you come by with your boats."

"Calm down," Virginia said, "until I'm used to the light."

MAY QUEEN

I SEE her skirt, Denise," Mickey said to his wife. "It's blue. I can't see her face because her head's lowered, but the two attendants with her are wearing gloves, right?"

He was standing on the hood of his new tan Lincoln Continental, in a parking space behind the crowds of parents outside St. Rose of Lima Church, in Indianapolis. He had one hand over his eyebrows, explorer style, against the brilliant noonday sun. He was trying to see their daughter, Riva, who had been elected May Queen by her senior high-school class, and who was leading students from all the twelve grades in a procession around the school grounds.

"There's a guy with balloons over there," Mickey said.

Denise stood with the small of her back leaning against one of the car headlights. Around her there were a good three or four hundred people, scattered in the parking lot and on some of the school's athletic fields. They held mimeographed hymn sheets, loose bunches of garden flowers, little children's hands. Some of the women wore straw hats with wide brims and some of the men wore visored golf hats, against the sun, which was cutting and white, gleaming on car chrome and flattening the colors of clothes.

Mickey and Denise had been late getting started, and then Mickey had had trouble parking. "It's a damn good thing that the nuns picked Riva up this morning," Denise had said. "We'd have fritzed this whole thing."

Mickey moved cautiously along the hood of the Lincoln and jumped to the ground. "They're headed our way," he said. "They're past the elementary annex and rounding the backstops."

Denise said, "How does she look, Mick? Scared?"

"Sharp," Mickey said. "Right in step."

"I know," Denise said, clapping her hands. "I love that dress, if I do say so."

"I keep forgetting it was your handiwork," Mickey said.

Denise pushed her glasses up on her nose and made a mad face. Her glasses had lenses that magnified her eyes. "So is this, you forget," she said, pinching the bodice of her dress. She stood away so Mickey could admire her sleeveless green shift and the matching veil pinned in her shining gray hair.

After a while she said, "You know, three other parishes are having May processions today. I don't care. Ours is best. Ours is always the best, though I do like the all-men's choir at St. Catherine's."

"Mi-mi-mi," Mickey sang, and Denise elbowed him.

"Shhh," she said. "There they are."

"So grown up," Mickey said. "I ought to be hanged for leaving the movie camera at work Friday."

Altar boys with raised crucifixes headed the march, and behind them came a priest in a cassock and surplice, swinging a smoking bulb of incense. Riva came next, flanked by two boy attendants, who held the hem of her short cape. Beneath the cape Riva wore a blue bridesmaid's frock. She carried a tiny wreath of roses and fern on a satin pillow. Her face was lifted in the white light. Her throat moved as she sang the Ave Maria.

A family of redheads who were grouped ahead of Denise and Mickey turned around and grinned. Mickey wagged his head left and right. "Great!" he said.

Denise slipped a miniature bottle of spray perfume from her pocketbook. "One of us smells like dry-cleaning fluid," she said. She wet her wrists with the perfume. "Unless I'm reacting to the incense."

"It's me, I'm afraid," Mickey said. "This suit's been in

storage nine months." He brought his coat sleeve to his face and sniffed. "Maybe not. I don't know. Who cares? Let's enjoy the damn ceremony."

The procession had moved into the church and most of the people went in, too. Mickey and Denise threaded quickly through the crowd to the church doors. Mickey took the handle of Denise's pocketbook and guided her skillfully, but when they got inside the church, all the pew seats had been taken. They stood in back, in the center aisle, directly in front of the tabernacle. Riva was way up in front, kneeling between her attendants at the altar railing. The children's choir began a hymn about the month of May and the mother of Christ.

When the hymn was over, a young boy all in white got up on a stool near the front of the church and sang alone. Riva and her attendants got off their knees and moved to the left of the altar, where a stepladder, draped in linen and hung with bouquets, had been positioned next to a statue of the Virgin Mary. The arms of the statue extended over a bay of burning candles in supplication.

Riva climbed the stepladder, still carrying the wreath on the satin pillow. She faced the church crowd and held the wreath high. Mickey and Denise grabbed hands. Riva's eyes were raised. She turned and began to place the wreath over the Virgin's head.

"Am I right?" a man standing next to Mickey said. "Her dress looks like it's caught fire."

"Dress is on fire!" someone said loudly. There was quiet, and then there was noise in the church. People half-stood in their pews. A young priest hurried to Riva. She was batting at her gown with the satin pillow. The fern wreath wheeled in the air. Her attendants pulled her down the steps of the ladder.

Mickey shouted, "Stop!" and ran for the altar. He pushed people out of the way. "I'm her dad," he said.

The priest had Riva by both shoulders, pressed against him. He folded her in the apron of his cassock, and a white flame broke under his arm.

"They *both* caught," a woman in front of Mickey said.

The priest smothered Riva's flaring skirt. He looked left and right and said, "Everybody stay back." Riva collapsed on the priest's arm and slid toward the floor.

Mickey vaulted over a velvet cord in front of the altar. He and the priest picked up Riva and between them carried her quickly across the altar and through a doorway that led into the sacristy.

An usher with a lily dangling from the lapel of his suit jacket came into the room with a folded canvas cot. "Put her here," he said. "Just a minute. Just one minute." He unfolded the cot, yanking at the stiff wooden legs. "There she goes," he said.

When they got Riva lying down, an older priest, in vestments, began sending people away from the room. Denise was allowed in. She helped Mickey cover Riva's charred dress with a blanket.

"That leg is burned," the first priest said. "Don't cover it up."

"I'm sorry," Denise said.

The two priests sat facing each other in metal chairs, as if they were playing a card game.

"We called for an ambulance, Father," the usher said to both of them.

"It doesn't look too terrible," Mickey said as he folded the burned skirt back and examined his daughter's leg. He glanced around at the priests. "I think we're going to be okay here," he said.

Riva was sobbing softly.

Denise stood at the base of the cot and clutched each of Riva's white slippers.

"Listen, sweetheart," Mickey said, "your parents are right here. It's just a little burn, you know. What they call first degree, maybe."

Riva said nothing.

"When this thing is over," Mickey said, "and you're taken care of — listen to me, now — we'll go up to Lake Erie, okay? You hear me? How about that? Some good friends of mine, Tad Austin and his wife — you never met them, Riva — have an A-frame on the water there. We can lie around and bake in the sun all day. There's an amusement park, and you'll be eighteen then. You'll be able to drink, if you want to."

The priests were looking at Mickey. He blotted perspiration from his forehead with his coat sleeve.

Denise said, "I'm surprised they are not here yet." Her glasses had fallen off and she was crying with her mouth open, still holding Riva's feet.

"Give them a little longer," one of the priests said.

"You know," Mickey said to Riva, "something else I just thought of. Tad's wife will be at Erie some of the time. Remember how I told you about her? She's the one who went on television and won a convertible."

"Will you shut up?" Riva said.

BUD PARROT

H E W A T C H E D the new bride from across a banquet table where punch cups were cluttered, napkins, an ice swan, the high remains of a many-tiered cake.

It was a cool late-September noon. The bride's name was Gail, and she had pulled on a babyish short-sleeved sweater over her strapless, backless wedding dress. Bud Parrot was looking at her arms.

A hundred people were at the reception on the broad lawn behind the bride's father's house, in Ohio, in East Columbus, in Bexley. There were working fountains on the lawn, to the right and left of a rose garden. There was a waxed platform for dancing, and two loudspeakers wired to a sound system in the house. They were booming a big-band jitterbug song. A man in a frilled-front shirt and white jacket was spinning clownishly, alone on the platform. The bridal car, a milky Mercedes, was parked on the grass.

The bride's older sister, a brunette in yellow, was dish-toweling a puddle from the bar table. She dropped a lime disk into a cocktail, hesitated, then fished the fruit out and threw it on the ground. She handed the drink to Bud Parrot.

"Another one," Bud said. "Thanks."

"I'm a good barmaid," the brunette said.

"You're the bride's sister, aren't you? Aren't you Evaline?"

"Yeah," Evaline said. "Which side are you on? The bride's or the groom's?"

"Both. I know both of them," Bud said. "I'm older friends with Dean than Gail. By about thirty minutes."

Evaline stood over bottles of various kinds of liquor. She stirred up a warm martini and handed it to Bud Parrot.

"One for both hands," he said. "Thanks."

Evaline began to make a Gibson. "What's your name?" she said. "Maybe I've heard of you."

Bud said, "Bud."

"Oh," Evaline said, looking a bit flustered. "Oh, yeah."

Gail Redding Blaines, the bride, hitched up her skirt and crossed the dance platform on her way over to Bud. She made a V with her fingers and patted her lips. Bud tapped some cigarettes onto the bar table.

"I only need one," Gail said, sounding out of breath and excited. "Hi," she said to her sister. "You've met Buddy-boy, eh?" She put a cigarette to her lips.

A weathered man of at least sixty came forward to light the bride's cigarette. The man struck a stick match on the zippered fly of his dress trousers. He stood in front of Gail with his feet planted wide apart for balance.

"Daddy-boy," Gail said, inhaling.

The man waved out the match and tossed it into a punch cup. He looked without pleasure over the crowd on his lawn. "That fathead Ed Byers," he said. "That bufflehead."

Gail smiled at Bud. She said to her father, "Were you arguing again, Daddy?"

"You don't argue with Ed Byers," the man said. "You try to fit two words in sidewise."

Bud said, "The worst used car I ever bought in my life came from an Ed Byers lot."

Mr. Redding looked at Bud. He said to Gail, "Who is this?"

Gail introduced Bud Parrot.

"You a friend of the groom's?"

"He's a mutual friend," Gail said. "Dean and Bud and I met on the same night, didn't we? At a party that we all decided to leave because it was so boring — right, Bud?"

Bud had some of his drink and said, "Right." He looked at Evaline, who was slopping Scotch whisky into a glass. She winked at him.

Evaline said, "Bud and Dean roomed together in college, or something."

"College and after," the bride said. "You've met Bud before, Dad."

"I don't remember," Mr. Redding said.

Evaline winked at Bud again and then at her sister and then once more at Bud.

"I remember," said a woman with a yellow net hat and dark glasses. She was sitting in a too-short chair about ten yards from them, facing the lawn. She had a plate with a wedge of cake on her lap and one of Evaline's tall, sweating highballs in her right hand. "I remember Bud," she said. "Don't I, Bud?"

"Mother remembers," Evaline said, smiling and winking at Bud again and then winking at the back of her father's head and finally at the cup of Scotch in her hand.

Bud emptied his glass and excused himself. He asked Gail's mother to dance.

On the platform, Mrs. Redding's step was serious. She kept her neck stiff as she dipped, humming in her throat.

Bud delivered her back to her short chair. Mr. Redding was standing by the chair, legs spread.

"You working?" he said to Bud.

"I live over East," Bud began, "and I'm on leave of absence."

But Mr. Redding had wheeled around and was saying, "Hey, Evvy! We don't need chairs," to Evaline, who was dragging a picnic bench over to them.

The bride, Gail, rejoined them. She kissed her father and

her mother and then she looked at the sky. "Is that the sun or the moon?" she said. "I can't tell."

"Sun," Bud said.

Gail puffed on her cigarette and tipped her head back. She and Bud watched the smoke rope upward and disperse. Bud said to her, in a low voice, "Do I have to tell you you're, uh, radiant? You look absolutely — "

"I've heard all that," Gail said. "But, boy, do *you* look good."

"I do?" Bud said.

"Did you know the brown tuxedos were my idea? And you are perfect for brown, Bud. I mean it."

"Your mother's asleep," Bud said. They looked at Mrs. Redding, whose cheek was pushed fatly against her shoulder.

Mr. Redding was propped, arms folded, with his back pressed on a thick maple tree. "She's having a good time," he said. "Have some of that million-dollar cake, Evvy. We're going to have to chuck it out if someone doesn't eat."

Evaline was drinking furiously from the cup of Scotch. The air was breezy and there were green and gold leaves in the yard, but Evaline had droplets of perspiration on the end of her nose. "There are eighty thousand people here to eat the cake," she said. "I don't want any. No cake for me."

"That's smart," Mr. Redding said. "You watch your figure."

"I am," she said, and winked at him.

"C'mon, Mommy," Mr. Redding said to his sleeping wife. "Let's head for coffee."

When he had helped his wife get up and the two of them had moved off, Evaline said, "I can't stand them. Especially I can't stand him."

Bud rolled his eyes in the direction of Gail, who was not far away, doing a mock-serious tango with Evaline's youngest child, ten-year-old Tucker.

"I don't care," Evaline said. "Gail can't stand them, either — hey, can you, Gail?"

"Nope," Gail said, marching Tucker straight toward a privet hedge.

Dean Blaines, the groom, came up the walk from the rose garden. Trailing him was a photographer strapped with cameras. The photographer took some pictures, and Dean held out the flared skirt of his tailored tuxedo jacket and performed turns. Dean was dark and attractive, with an involuntary-sounding laugh that showed his white teeth and kept him busy most of the time.

Bud studied Dean's chewed fingernails and the many cuts on his hands from his work at the lumberyards and paneling centers he owned in town.

"Well, Bud," Dean said, "it's a wedding." He said to the photographer, "Get some snaps of Bud." He said to Evaline, "Somebody better cut you back on the drinks, Evvy. Your eye-twitching could be taken for an invitation."

"Hey, Mrs. Blaines," Dean said to his new bride, "have you danced with Bud?"

"He won't want to," Gail said.

"I don't want to," Bud said. "I mean, I don't dance."

"See?" Gail said. "Besides, I've got a fellow." She mussed Tucker's hair.

Bud went over to where some people were milling in a corner of the lawn. A man of about fifty, very pale, was lying flat on his back. Mr. Redding was there, with a thick cheroot stuck in his mouth.

"Everybody quiet down," he was saying. He weaved

slightly and took off his dress jacket and dropped it on the ground. He ran his thumbs up and down the insides of his white suspenders. "He had too much punch," Mr. Redding said to Bud. "Let's clear off before he starts to be sick."

Bud pulled his jacket off, too, and folded it over his arm and walked with Mr. Redding up seventy-five yards of lawn to a rectangle of Cyclone fence that encircled clay tennis courts and an emerald-painted swimming pool.

"Dip?" Mr. Redding said. He put all his weight against the chain-link fence and wound his fingers in the wire diamonds. "We're draining it tomorrow."

"No," Bud said.

"What can we do for you?" Mr. Redding said. "What can we do so you'll enjoy the wedding? Short of an annulment."

Bud looked surprised. "I'm enjoying it," he said. "A lot." The older man turned around. He smelled of alcohol and faintly of the cedar closet where his clothes came from.

"Bud?"

"Um-hmm?"

"What I think is the most beautiful wild flower, the fringed gentian. You can barely see it peeking around the diving tower. See it?"

"Mmm," Bud said. He was crouched against the fence in the shadow of the tower, fingering the fine silt of an anthill.

"Come on now," Mr. Redding said. "Get back to earth."

"I'm on earth," Bud said, with his nose full.

"I had to see a girlfriend of mine get married. I had to be the damned best man. It tore me up. But a year later I met Gail's mother and a year after that the first couple were divorced and I didn't even give a curse."

Bud was laughing weakly.

"You've never married," Mr. Redding said. "You're not

very much to look at."

"No," Bud said.

"You're bright, though. And because of that, bored."

"That's it on the nose," Bud said.

Around three, Bud got his Opel out of the sun and drove it into some shade being thrown by the branches of a walnut tree. He sat in the car, watching the grounds next to the Reddings' — a school for girls. Some teen-agers were having a softball game there, throwing up dust as they swung and missed and took off for first base anyway.

Bud got the key to his glove compartment from where it was secured to the sun visor with a rubber band. He looked for paper and finally ripped a blank page from the back of his car-service manual.

"This is the last letter you'll get from me, Dean," Bud wrote before his fountain pen clogged. He removed the ink cartridge and shook it. A bubble of blue rolled along his wrist and some blue plips appeared on the bib of his dress shirt. Exasperated, he lit a cigarette and smeared ink on his mouth. He licked his palm and was pressing it along his lips when Evaline came around the walnut tree.

She stopped, a few feet from Bud's window.

"Damn it," he said, licking at the ink.

Evaline jumped. "Jesus," she said. "I didn't see you there. You almost gave me a heart attack." She stooped and looked in at Bud. "Help me find my shoe, will you? It's out here somewhere."

"In a minute," Bud said.

"Forget it," Evaline said. She went around and got into the car. "Let me just sit here a second. I'm feeling — you know."

"I know," Bud said. "Me, too."

"What happened to you?" she asked.

"Ink," Bud said. "Everybody leaving?"

"Mostly," Evaline said. "Except for some people dumping out the ashtrays and putting away folding chairs. I forgot your first name."

"Bud."

"I need air, Bud. How about driving us around?"

"Will you slow down? I'm trying to light this cigarette. This is the second time I've burned myself," Evaline said.

"It's not me," Bud said. "It's this road."

They bucketed over a pothole and landed in the dirt yard of a cinder-block house where there was rusting lawn furniture and a sign that read NO CHRISTMAS TREES.

"A good neighborhood," Evaline said. "A good road."

"Hold your britches," Bud said. "I'm going for the Outerbelt. I was thinking we could go to the amusement park out by the zoo."

"Well, that's crazy," Evaline said. "I've got to be back to stow my kids in bed."

"It's a good place to go," Bud said. "It's on the river, all lit up with colored lightbulbs. There's a merry-go-round, Ferris wheel, a good roller coaster. It's wood."

"I've been to the zoo park," Evaline said.

"You've got some time," Bud said. "Let's go anyway."

They stood under the Zipper Ride, which turned people in cages upside down, and Evaline found things that had dropped from pockets and purses. She found a snapped pair of glasses with mirror lenses, a Canadian coin, an inch of ball chain.

Music ground from the stationary vintage merry-go-round. The wooden roller coaster slammed and clattered, its only passenger a seven- or eight-year-old girl.

Bud shot an air rifle in a plywood stall that was hung with purple and turquoise dogs. "Good," the booth's owner said. "You didn't hit anything."

"Come and ride the Spider," a boy said to Evaline. "Come on. The last ride of the season."

"What does the Spider do?" she asked.

"You laugh," the boy said, wiping a lot of black hair off his forehead, "or I let you off if you're not laughing."

"No, I don't think so," Evaline said.

She waited at a concessions trailer while Bud went into the deserted penny arcade and started playing a pinball machine. She followed him in after a while, and sat on an air-hockey table and watched the steel bearings Bud fired around. Lights ignited, sounding bells and buzzers. Bud looked serious over the machine. He used his thigh to jostle the thing.

"Believe it or not, I'm hungry," Evaline said. "I can't get anyone to wait on me out there."

The score tabulator on the pinball machine whirred and clucked.

Bud said, "Forty-seven thousand eight hundred."

He took Evaline back to the empty concessions trailer and they waited under the awning some more.

"See?" she said. "Nobody comes."

The trailer had hampers of popcorn, and dark globes of syrup for snow cones. There were frankfurters, which were skewered on a revolving wire tree, glistening from a glass box. Bud jumped up onto the service counter and lowered himself into the food mobile. "Help you?" he said.

"Hey," Evaline said. "You look good there."

Bud made Coney Islands, and folded up a candy-striped box and filled it with popcorn. He drew sodas into big waxed cups.

"I've seen it all," said an enormous woman who had an apron cinched under her enormous bosom. She laughed, and the flesh around her throat and belly jiggled. She looked at Evaline's feet, which were in shredded hose, and she laughed.

"We were going to pay," Bud said.

"Oh, I know you'll pay," the woman said.

Bud hefted himself, with straight arms, out of the booth, and dropped beside Evaline. He paid the woman from his wallet.

They walked along the darkened midway. Evaline said, "Uh-oh." A legless man on a cart steered up to them. On the back of the cart was a perfectly square pile of newspapers.

"Hey, *Dispatch*," the legless man said, and Bud bought an evening paper from him. The man rolled away, guiding the cart with two rubber doughnuts.

"I'm freezing," Evaline said.

Bud leaned to have her repeat the sentence. A wind was blowing leaves across the park and horns were bleating from the Flying Bobs ride.

"I am *cold*," Evaline said, loudly.

"It's nice, isn't it?" Bud said. "Let's go see Dean and Gail."

"Grandma Redding tucked in my kids," Evaline said.

"Who tucked in Grandma Redding?" Bud said.

Evaline looked at her thin watch. "It's close to nine-thirty. It's too late."

"You can wait here," Bud said. "I'll buy you a magazine. Or you can go up with me."

They were in the lobby of the Hilton Hotel, on State Street. Evaline had just left a line of telephone booths and she stood with Bud outside the hotel's bar. She bunched her toes in the scarlet carpet.

"I don't think this is all right," she said.

Bud went over to one of the desk clerks, a startled-looking bald man in a fiery orange coat.

"Are you coming?" he said to Evaline. "It's room 1410 and they *want* to see us. I had him call up and announce us."

Evaline went with Bud to an elevator with chromed walls. Bud squeezed his eyes shut against their reflection — he with beard shadow and ink-spattered clothes; Evaline dusty, red-eyed, barefoot.

The doors sluiced open on the fourteenth floor, opposite a thigh-high ceramic bowl of ostrich feathers.

Dean Blaines answered the door of room 1410. He wore a short silk robe decorated with black and yellow butterflies. He showed Bud his biggest smile and then he said, "Come in and have a look. It's a suite."

"My," Evaline said. She nodded at her sister, who was still in her wedding gown, sitting cross-legged on the tightly made bed, which was under a glassed Degas reproduction. She was watching a quiz show on the hotel television.

"We came busting in on you," Evaline said. "On your wedding night. It's ridiculous to be here."

"Oh, hell, Evvy," Gail said. "Sit down and shut up about wedding nights."

"Yeah, Evvy," Dean said. "This isn't 1920 or anything. The honeymoon will start, we decided, when we get to Madrid."

"Or whenever," the bride said. "This is just another night in Columbus to me. To us. Have you two been in a pie fight or something?"

Bud, who had been standing by a low bureau that was covered with vases of flowers, poked his finger in the cellophane that covered a fruit basket. He took an apple from where it was nestled in green excelsior. "Hey, Dean," he said, "let's go for a little spin down the hall. Two minutes."

"Dean's all settled in — with his robe and all," Gail said.

"This is wonderful," Evaline said. "It's so big, you could get lost trying to track down the bathroom." She left the big bedroom.

"I don't think the *bride* should say this," Gail said, "but that was the most perfect wedding I ever went to." She looked at Bud.

"Milt Pilsney drank himself flat on his back," Dean said.

"Evvy was so funny," Gail said. She had not moved her eyes from Bud.

"Dean," Bud said. "Please."

"I won't let her take the dress off," Dean said. "It's so terrific. Honestly, Gail," he said to his wife. "It looks really, really good."

"Why, thank you, Dean," Gail said.

Evaline came out of the bathroom cradling a white puppy who was making a little bark.

"Shut up, Pietro," Gail said to the dog. "Throw him

down, Evaline, if he bothers you. Or keep him. He was a wedding present."

"We're going to Spain!" Dean said. "Bud, can you believe it?"

"No," Bud said. He used his teeth on the apple he had taken from the fruit basket. "I can't believe you want to go to Spain. In the first place, you won't believe how dirty it is. How cruel and stupid the people are, or how punishing the sun."

"Okay," Gail said, closing her eyes. "Okay, okay, okay."

"We'll like it in Spain," Dean said. "If nothing else, just for the flamenco."

Evaline did a little flamenco dance, drumming her bare heels on the rug and working imaginary castanets in her hands.

"I must be nuts," she said, stopping the dance.

Bud, who was chewing his apple, said, "Olé. Dean, I came all the way down here."

"We appreciate it," Dean said. He put himself on the bed beside Gail, who was still looking, very hard, at Bud.

Dean began, absently, to rub Gail's naked back. "I'm ecstatic," he said. "I'm really too excited to sleep. You know, in thirty-five years I've never been out of this country once?"

SMOKE

MARTY BAKER followed his mother's car through Beverly Hills. But she was too good a driver for Marty to stay close, even on his motorcycle. The remarried Mrs. Audry Baker Sharon caught the last corner before her new home, going sixty at the apex of the curve, tires grounded, exhaust pipes firing like pistol shots.

She was laughing, leaning out the driver's door of her car, brushing sand stains from her toasted feet, when Marty drove his bike onto the blacktop turnaround. He dropped his kickstand, sat sideways on the bike saddle, and lighted a cigarette. He was twenty-six, wearing Levi's, suspenders, no shirt, and linesman's boots.

His mother said, "I won. You couldn't catch me, and you had all the way from Santa Monica."

"I had all the way from Malibu," Marty said. "I saw you leaving the Mayfair Market. You made every single light, though. I had to stop a lot."

Audry Sharon hefted a paper sack of groceries and a cluster of iced tea cans from the passenger seat of her sports car. She cradled the groceries in her arm, hooked the cans with her free fingers, used her knee to slam the car door, and came toward Marty.

"Give us a puff," she said.

Marty put his cigarette between his mother's lips. "I need to borrow a great deal of money," he said while Audry inhaled, "before the weekend."

"Don't talk to me," she said. "Talk to Hoyt."

Marty wiggled his jaw and yanked at his chin strap. He lifted off his motorcycle helmet. "I can't talk to Hoyt," he said.

Hoyt Sharon came around from the side lawn, carrying a nine iron and a whiffle golf ball. His white hair was shaved to a fine bristle on his head and he wore what looked to Marty like a crimson spacesuit — one-piece, with the Velcro closing strips undone from his throat to his midbelly.

"Marty! Great! Come in, come in," Hoyt said.

"Hey," Marty said, "how's the honeymoon?"

Hoyt had planted himself over the golf ball. He rolled his shoulders and swung the club. The ball clicked and shot straight onto the shingled slant of the garage roof. "So much for *that* soldier," Hoyt said. He came up behind Audry, and tried to take the groceries away from her.

"Will you please calm down?" she said to him. "Look at how much you're sweating."

"Okay. Sorry," Hoyt said.

Audry said, "If you want to help me carry, get the food cooler and beach umbrella from the trunk."

"Remember to talk to him for me," Marty whispered to his mother as they trailed Hoyt around the side of the house.

Hoyt hurried ahead, dumped the umbrella and golf club he was toting, and opened doors for Audry and Marty.

They entered a paneled foyer that was cluttered with plants and old, bright oil paintings of sinewy cowboys.

Audry went up a short, carpeted stairs and through a swinging saloon door.

Hoyt led Marty through the game room with the emerald carpet and billiards table, through the oval room, which was being papered with flocked maroon sheets, to a big library. The library was two stories tall and had a row of theater seats bolted to one wall, a sofa as long and deep as a small boat, which was sunk in a pit area, a back wall of sliding glass, and a ten-foot mural depicting a cattle stampede and a man being flung from the saddle of a panicky-looking horse.

Marty sat in an armchair that had been branded with dozens of ranch logos.

Hoyt leaped into the sunken pit area and tossed himself on the boat-sized couch. He clasped his hands behind his head. "Your mom tell you about Henry Kissinger?" he said. "It's the damnedest thing. She tell you? You won't believe it."

"I don't think so," Marty said. "No."

"Ben Deverow and his wife — you don't know them — go into the Derby for lunch and there he is, Henry Kissinger."

"Really?" Marty said.

"Yeah, having shrimp or something," Hoyt said. "Only — you won't believe this, but he's in drag. He's dressed up like a woman."

"Oh, come on," Marty said, reaching across the coffee table for a *Sports Illustrated.*

"No. He's really Kissinger, but he's got a — a whatchumacallit — " Hoyt pointed to the swordfish stitched on his billed cap.

"A wig?"

"No, he didn't even have a wig. He had a little — like a hat thing, you know? With a little lace veil?"

Marty said, "He couldn't do that. Everyone would know if he dressed up like a woman and went out in public."

"That's what you'd think," Hoyt said. "It's what I'd think, isn't it? But it was him. I swear it."

"You weren't even there," Marty said.

"Isn't that incredible about Henry Kissinger?" Audry said as she padded into the room. She had put on a pair of jeans, and fixed her hair in a thick ponytail.

Hoyt excused himself and took a dark Spansule from his shirt pocket. He put the pill on his tongue, hopped from the couch area, crossed the room, and gulped from a cut-glass decanter.

Marty cleared his throat and turned the pages of his magazine.

"Oh, yeah," Audry said. She folded her knees and sat on her heels in front of a console-model television. "Marty needs money for his business, Hoyt."

Hoyt said, "Why the hell didn't he come to me before?" He slapped his palms on the seat of his spacesuit.

"He didn't need money before," Audry said.

"Look," Hoyt said, "I get a kick out of helping young people. You know who helped me when I was stalled? Forty years ago, when Anaheim was just a crop and a half of orange trees?"

"Gene Autry," Audry said.

"Gene Autry," Hoyt said, "is who. That's right, honey." He turned to Marty and said, "No, I don't see any problem here. What are we playing with? Land?"

"Smoke detectors," Marty said. "I can get in on a pretty safe operation, Hoyt. Some friends in Sacramento tell me they're thinking about making detectors mandatory by the next decade."

"Besides which I believe in the damn things," Hoyt said. "They're like little alarms? You bet I do. They save lives. Friends of mine lost a kid in a fire once. I say a kid, but I mean infant. You should have seen it." He parted his hands. "They had a teeny casket only this big."

Audry switched on the television and tuned in a local charity telethon. A high-school orchestra was introduced and started playing "High Hopes." Hoyt looked interested in the show, and sat on the carpet beside his wife.

"Can I neck with you for a second?" the show's emcee

said to a five-year-old whose legs were strapped with metal braces. The child had on a party dress. "Why can't I?" the emcee said. "Are you married?" He dropped on one knee before the girl and squinted at her suspiciously.

"No, I'm too little," the child said.

"You aren't too little," the emcee told her, and smiled at the audience. "You're one of the very biggest people on this planet, because your heart is full of courage and hope."

Marty blinked, and got up and went to the double glass doors. He moved them easily on their runners. There was the smell of cut grass, the knock of a carpenter's hammer, the hiss of lawn sprinklers.

Audry switched off the television. She reached for the telephone and called in a pledge of three thousand dollars to the charity show.

Hoyt rose and headed across the room. He sprang on the balls of his feet, shooting fists in combinations. "Okay, buddy," he said to Marty. "Your turn. Waltz with me a few rounds."

"I really can't, Hoyt," Marty said.

"You want a grubstake?" Hoyt said. "You got to do a little dancing."

He moved easily, but his face was purpling. He jabbed, wide of Marty's throat, with the pointed second-joint knuckles of his fingers.

Audry hung up the telephone and watched with her arms folded in front of her.

Hoyt stopped moving. Marty stood before him, flat-footed, his arms half-raised.

"The old monkey," Hoyt said.

He swung a clowning roundhouse right that smashed into Marty's left temple.

"Jesus, Hoyt," Marty said.

The blow had knocked him onto his hip.

"He's all right," Hoyt said to Audry.

"I'm all right," Marty said, getting to his feet.

Hoyt danced toward him.

"Cover up," Hoyt said, and Marty crouched and crossed his arms over his face.

"Breadbasket," Hoyt said, and whipped his left fist at Marty's bare stomach.

Marty walked away, with his hands on his hips, looking for a breath. He collapsed to a squat.

"Leave him alone," Audry said. "Poor Marty."

"Christ, Hoyt," Marty said.

"Woozy?" Audry asked him. She made Marty get on all fours and she put a wastepaper can under his face.

"I'm sorry, Marty," Hoyt said. "That was nuts of me. Just wanted to get the blood headed back to the pump, you know? Those weren't supposed to land."

"You didn't have to put his eye out," Audry said.

"I think he did," Marty said. "I can't see out of it."

"Look at me," Audry said, taking Marty's chin in her hand. "No. All it is is a sliver cut at the edge of the brow. You'll have a mouse that may close your eye a bit. I'll get you a cup of coffee." She left the room.

Marty sat on the ottoman. Hoyt paced in front of him.

"Forget it, Hoyt," Marty said. "Really."

"I didn't mean for those to land. You're a great kid for not hauling off and plastering me right back."

Marty said, "I wouldn't mess with you."

"What'd you say you'd need to get in on those alarm systems? Did you say three or four thousand?"

"Really, three thousand is more than it would take,"

Marty said. "Three thousand is great, sir."

"Not 'sir.' Don't call me 'sir.' " Hoyt went back to the couch in the sunken pit. He pounded his chest a few times. He put a finger on the side of his nose, closing off the nostril, and breathed deeply five or six times. "Listen, though," he said. "Don't those smoke alarms sometimes go off when there's no fire?"

"They're working on perfecting that," Marty said.

"Your mother's so mad at me," Hoyt said.

"I'll tell her everything's okay," Marty said.

"Everything's all right here," Hoyt said when Audry came back into the room. She was carrying a saucer and a full china cup for Marty. She and Marty smiled at one another. When Marty glanced over at Hoyt, Marty saw that Hoyt was grinning, too.

"Here's the big plan," Hoyt said. "My father told me the only things you got to worry about are sex, death, and taxes. And he told me, but if you've got the right family, you'll never have to worry."

INDEPENDENCE
DAY

HELEN had not done anything all June. She did not have to. Nothing was required of her. Her estranged husband was in Detroit somewhere. Her retired father was housing her in a grand stone house in Port Brent, a lakeside resort town in northern Ohio. The house was on a cove and the backyard led to a private pier where Helen's father moored his boats, an old wooden Chris-Craft with an Evinrude engine, and a Lido sailboat.

It was not good for Helen, having nothing to do. If you didn't do things to your life, she decided, it would begin doing things to you. She decided this while lying in bed at four-thirty in the morning. She was looking at her knees, and, as if to confirm her thought, she heard a clunk sound that she recognized as the air conditioner breaking down.

She turned onto her side.

She woke up sweating at one o'clock the next afternoon, and stepped into some beach thongs and a sundress. It was almost a hundred degrees in her third-story room.

Down in the kitchen, her sister, Darla, who was twenty-five, had her elbows splayed on the open morning newspaper; she was reading Maggie and Jiggs.

Helen peeled an orange over the kitchen counter and considered her sister, who was sweating, too, in an immodest calico bikini. Darla snorted a laugh through her nose at the paper, then raised her eyes to stare at a hose that connected the dishwashing machine.

Darla had a cottage somewhere on the lake, but she was

an in-and-out visitor at the Kenning house. Since May, she had been mostly an "in" visitor, as she was low on money and boyfriends.

"Where's Father?" Helen said.

Darla nodded toward a backfiring engine noise out the window.

Helen lifted herself on her toes and looked through the double windows over the sink. She saw her father on his riding mower, in the west stretch of the lawn. He and the mower were bounding over the crest of a little slope.

Helen said, "Why isn't he fixing the air conditioner? Why is he mowing the lawn?"

Darla shrugged, studying the washing instructions on the inside of her swimsuit's bra cup.

"I'm getting sick," Helen said. "I'm going to get Father."

"Terry called," Darla said. She moved a butter plate and some juice glasses around on the table so she could roll the paper over.

Terry, Helen's husband, had been calling from Detroit five times a day. Helen refused to talk to him because he usually had only one point to make, and that was that she should clear out of her father's place and get her own apartment.

She walked around the counter to the windowed aluminum door that led onto the patio and yard. Art Kenning had U-turned his mower and was charging for the house.

He eased the machine onto the patio's gravel apron. A pebble flew from the grass blower and stabbed the side of a wooden toolbox that was on the ground. "I thought that was a bullet," Mr. Kenning said, staring at the chip of stone. He said, "Your husband called this morning."

"What's wrong with the air conditioner?" Helen said,

over the idling of the engine. "Can't you fix it?"

"No," Mr. Kenning said, and sighed. "You'll have to live , without it."

"I can't live without it," Helen said.

"I'll look at it," Mr. Kenning said. "But I'm leaving in fifteen minutes. Where's your sister?"

"Inside," Helen said.

Her father stopped the engine and leaned back on the mower's saddle. He brought his feet up one by one and removed his shoes and socks. He stuffed the socks into the shoes and climbed down and picked his way, barefooted, over the gravel.

Helen followed him back into the kitchen, and they stood looking at Darla and the pattern on the tablecloth for a minute.

"This is Communism," Darla said, rapping a column in her newspaper. "I think we whipped the wrong damn army."

Mr. Kenning said, "You know, girls, this is a workday for most people."

"Tomorrow's Fourth of July," Darla said. "Not a work-day. So you'd better get a repairman out here." She wet the tip of her finger and turned a newspaper page. "Helen, get me a Coke while you're over there."

"Watch the handle on the refrigerator," Mr. Kenning said. "It's falling off."

Helen swam in the cove.

She and Darla rode the house bike, an old Schwinn, along the beach road. Helen pedaled, standing, while Darla sat on the bike's narrow seat with her pelvis thrust forward, her legs dangling, a cigarette in her hand.

After they swam, they lay side-by-side in the sun on the dock, their hair wrapped in colored towels.

"What are you writing?" Darla said, with her eyes closed. "I hear you writing."

"A book of days," Helen said. She had a sheaf of papers in a folder that she had brought along in the bike basket. She was flipping through the papers. She paused and scribbled with a red Flair pen.

"About Terry?" Darla said.

"Why would I write about Terry?"

"I don't know," Darla said. "What else have you got to write about? You don't date. You don't work. A book of days is supposed to be autobiography — about things happening. What's been happening to you?"

"I've got plenty in my life besides Terry," Helen said, but after a while she closed the folder, which contained mostly notes on movies and TV shows she had seen.

Helen swam again in the early evening. She brushed her wet blond hair into a spike and put on the same sundress. She walked a quarter mile of shady road through the resort town of Port Brent. On the edge of the town was a lounge Helen liked that was called — from what Helen could gather from the pink neon sign that marked the place — Seafood Liquor.

The lights in the lounge flickered on as she entered, although it was only six o'clock. She passed a line of men at the bar who were watching a trunk-sized color television that showed a horse race. She passed the little placard on a stand that read: "Please wait to be seated," and went to her usual booth, in the rear, under a stuffed, board-mounted, varnished lobster.

"Double White Horse, neat," Helen said when the waitress came.

The waitress, a big-boned pretty girl in the gingham house uniform, brought the drink right away, on a round tray with a cork mat and a book of paper matches.

Helen's Detroit husband, Terry, came into the bar. He went to Helen's booth. He lay on the bench seat across from her, with his legs up and crossed at the knee.

"It's Crayola at the clubhouse turn," said the TV announcer. "Crayola by a length."

The men along the bar cheered and punched each other, pulled each other's clothing, rearranged their standing and seating positions.

"I suppose it means something that you can always find me," Helen said to her husband.

Terry put a hand under his dark glasses and rubbed his eyes. "No. It just means you always go to the same places."

The pretty waitress brought Terry a menu, and he said, "No. I don't need it. The Bosun's platter and two of those." He pointed at Helen's drink.

"When did you drive down from Detroit?" Helen said. "It's a horrible drive, I know. I've done it."

"Have you?"

"Once," Helen said.

Terry said, "I had to come down because you never answer the phone. You know how many times I've called?"

"I know. I'm sorry," Helen said. "It's just that so many times I pick up the phone and the caller hangs up, or asks, 'Who is this?' To *me!*"

"That's nuts," Terry said. "That isn't the real reason. You don't come to the phone because you don't want to talk about what I want to talk about."

"You do kind of play the same violin, Terry."

"Well, I've got a different violin," he said. "I need to talk to you." He settled his dark glasses back on his face. "Something good's happened."

"Yes?" Helen said.

"Silly Brat. Silly Brat. Blinko and Silly Brat at the rail," said the TV.

"It's my birthday," Terry said. "I'm thirty-three."

"Oh, God. It is. I forgot all about it," Helen said. "July third, of course. I'm so sorry. Is that what you've been calling about?"

He looked sourly at Helen, and took her drink and finished it.

"Something very nice has happened," he said.

"You got a job," Helen said.

"Never mind," Terry said. "Thank you," he told the waitress, who put two wide full glasses and some napkins on the table.

"I won the state lottery," he said. "Legally. I won twelve thousand dollars on a ticket I bought in Euclid."

Helen said, "You really did?" and Terry began to nod with his lower lip fastened by his upper teeth. "That's incredible. That's wonderful. That is good news. Congratulations. I should say so."

"Yep," he said. "But there's an angle. There's a strong possibility I'll win a lot more, Helen. I'm likely to come out of this a millionaire."

"How?" she said. "This is remarkable. You!"

"Friday," he said. "There's another drawing, between me and some other people — five of them — and one of us gets the million dollars."

"Jesus," Helen said.

"Yeah, really," Terry said. "But don't worry. I'll win."

"You probably will," Helen said. "Whew!"

"Anyway," Terry said, "I'm going to give you some money. Whether I win more or not. I want you to move out of your dad's house."

"Oh, no," Helen said. "Same old violin."

"I want you to move," Terry said.

"I'm fine there," Helen said.

"I want you to get your own apartment," Terry said. "You've never spent a single night alone in your whole life. You don't know the first thing about just day-to-day getting by — earning money."

"Why would I want to spend a night alone? My father has plenty of money."

"I want you to move," Terry said.

"I'm fine where I am," Helen said.

"Yes, but, Helen," he said. "Okay," he said. "When I win the million dollars, I'll just buy the place."

"You can't buy the place," Helen said. "It's our home. My father has boats there. It's where I was raised. My mother *died* there, in the laundry room."

"She had a stroke in the laundry room. She died in a hospital," Terry said. "I'll buy it, and kick you out. I'll evict you."

The waitress brought him a small porcelain plate with a powdered dinner roll and a tablet of butter between waxed-paper squares. On a larger plate was a bowl of salad.

"I'll need cutlery," Terry said to her.

"Sorry?" the waitress said.

"Oh," Terry said, "skip it. I'll eat this junk with my fingers."

He picked up some chunks of lettuce and wedged them into his mouth.

There was a motorist's inn, a circle of shingle-roofed, paint-blistered buildings around a blacktop court, where Terry had taken a cabin. Helen woke up there, on the morning of the Fourth of July, to a local explosion. The room was queerly lit. One tall ceramic lamp, smoothly sculpted into a seahorse shape, threw the illumination from a low-wattage light bulb onto a wall of cheap paneling, and there was a tiny window with white drapes. The room smelled faintly of gunpowder and of the refrigerated air that blew from the air conditioner.

Terry had left the TV on and from her pillow Helen watched about ten minutes of an Abbott and Costello movie.

She stretched and got out of bed. She put on her sundress and stepped out the door. The sky was white. There was a yard with some playground equipment behind the circle of cabins. It was hot, and Helen spotted Terry, shirtless, with some young boys. Terry was supervising the firing off of cherry bombs, Chinese twisters, sparklers, paper tubes that foamed and smoked and boomed.

The neighborhood dogs were barking. Terry shaded his eyes. "You're up," he said to Helen. "Good morning."

"How could I help being up?" she said. She went back inside and tried to fix her hair with a tin comb from her handbag. The only mirror in the cabin was over the bathroom sink and it was missing big chips of silvered surface. Helen bent at the knees to fit her face between two flaked-off, black sections.

Terry came up behind her. There was a boom from outside the cabin. It shook the single window in its mounting.

"Did you leave your fireworks with those kids?" Helen

said. "They'll blast off their thumbs and you'll spend your twelve thousand on some lawsuit."

"They aren't my thumbs," Terry said.

Terry took Helen to the Port Brent parade. They sat on the courthouse lawn, near the curb, and watched the floats and the high-school band pass by. A man on ten-foot stilts in an Uncle Sam outfit stalked over them. Helen waved up at him.

"How are you today, darling?" the man said. His face, under the tall striped hat, was tiny.

Darla, Helen's sister, was in the parade, in a beige Ford that was part of the automobile show. She looked sad and pale, perched on the hood of the car.

"She was dreading this," Terry said.

"Who was?" Helen said.

"Darla. She was dreading this. Your father made her do it, I guess," Terry said.

"How would you know?" Helen said.

"I talk to Darla," Terry said. "Whenever you don't answer. I've talked to her a lot about her life."

"Have you? And what else?" Helen said. She had trouble holding a match still to light a cigarette.

"I came down to see her once. Maybe I shouldn't be telling you this."

"No, it's all right, I guess," Helen said. "So you want to buy my father's house?"

"If he wants me to," Terry said. "I get the impression he does. He doesn't want the responsibility for the place anymore. But I don't mind the responsibility. I'll buy it up and kick you out."

"All right," Helen said.

HEART

Roy had his nice shoes propped on the next bleacher seat. His cap drooped over his ear. He was staring up into a cloudy wreath of overhead lighting. The cigarette filter between his fingers began to burn.

A young man on a seat ahead of Roy hunched forward, calling instructions through a bottomless cardboard cup to a girl on the ice rink. The girl was skating to a recording of *Slaughter on Tenth Avenue.* She wore a yellow leotard and dark stockings, and her hair was in ducktails.

Roy stamped out his cigarette end. A fat boy climbed on the deep stairs in the aisle. The boy cocked his mouth open and used a finger to jiggle a loose front tooth.

Roy lit his last cigarette and watched the girl skating. She glided to a near low wall, turned her feet sideways, and stopped. Her yellow leotard was wet, creased sharply above her thighs. She put her hands on her hips. She was having trouble breathing.

"Want to pack it in?" said the young man with the cup.

The girl nodded, swiveled her skates, and then went backward to a card table, which held up a portable record player. She lifted the needle arm.

"Alley oop," the young man called. "We don't mention those choppy turns," he said to Roy. "We're just here for the fun of it."

"I wouldn't know the difference," Roy said. "It looks so good."

Across the rink, the girl was hobbling on her skate blades along a strip of carpeting, toward a dressing locker.

"I used to see you skate together," Roy said.

"Where?" the young man said. He looked pleased. "Here?"

"That's right," Roy said.

"We used to practice together. We had some routines. I've got a little swelling in my knee." The young man tapped his right leg.

"Let's go look at the gray coat, can we?" the girl yelled from the far side of the rink.

"Let's go buy it for you," the young man yelled back.

Roy circled the big building on foot. He saw the fat boy with the loose tooth standing with a girl. The girl was a little older, taller than the boy. Her arm was twisted behind her back and pinned there by the fat boy's left hand. With his right hand, he was socking her on the shoulders and neck. It was August and dry and hot. But they were fighting in a six-foot cone of snow — scrapings from the rink.

Roy stopped walking and crossed his arms. The fat boy stepped away from the girl. He stretched his throat and looked sideways at Roy. The girl coughed.

Roy leaned against a wall. "Why hit her?" he said. "She's too pretty to hit." Out in the sun, in the snow, the two children looked Oriental. They had black hair and creamy brown skin. They stared at Roy in the flat green heat. Their black eyes were narrowed. The girl's mouth was open, her lower lip jutting.

"You speak English. Am I right?" Roy said.

The girl looked at the fat boy.

"English?" Roy said.

"We've never been outside this country," the boy said.

"My uncle was born here. I'm Frank Henderson."

"Why were you hitting her?" Roy said.

"She's my sister," Frank Henderson said.

The girl was rubbing her shoulder. Roy said to her, "He was hitting you."

"He's not a little gentleman," the girl said. She spoke with her face pointed at her running shoes.

Frank Henderson tipped over and used his hands to scoop snow. He wadded and packed an ice ball.

The girl raised an arm and covered her head. "If you do," she said.

"Here you go," Roy said, moving off the wall. He made a mitt with his hands. "Right here, Frank."

The ice ball went several feet wide of Roy.

"I've been out of the country," Roy said to them. "I lived in Italy and Greece. I can't get used to being back here. Greece was funny, though. You know where Greece is?" he said to the girl.

She said, "Yes."

The boy had another handful of snow. He was eating it and squinting at Roy. "I'm related to the manager here," the fat boy said. "They rent skates out to the public on weekdays, after four o'clock."

"I know that," Roy said. He studied the palm full of silver coins he had brought from his pocket. "I'd offer to buy you two a couple bottles of Coke, but I'm a nickel short."

"We have to work today," Frank Henderson said. "Don't you have work to do?" The boy patted his wet hands.

"Nope," Roy said.

"I hope you get to like living in America a little better," the boy said.

"Oh, no problem," Roy said, wagging his head.

The fat boy and his sister boarded a caged outside

elevator that was beside the pile of snow. They drove the machine underground.

Roy removed his new shoes and his socks. He walked along the curb of the broad avenue, carrying the shoes by their leather laces. "*Il tuci mi' amore dulce*," he sang. "*Il bidone' casa me strata*."

Roy sat on a big sofa he had moved onto his front porch. The porch was cement, shaded by an awning at the end of a short flight of cement steps that led to the sidewalk. Traffic on the street was thin.

"Wake up and live," Roy told a long red dog that lived in the neighborhood. The dog was on the sofa with Roy. "Count the Fords that pass."

"MacNamara!" Roy shouted to a newspaper boy pumping a yellow Schwinn that was strapped with saddlebags. The bike's front tire swerved. The rider went over onto the sidewalk. Roy came down from the porch.

"That always happens," MacNamara said. He had torn the flesh on an elbow. He was trying to straighten the handlebars.

"My fault," Roy said.

"Jesus," MacNamara said.

"Since you dropped it," Roy said, looking into MacNamara's face, "what do I owe you?"

The boy brought a tiny ring-binder from one of the saddlebags and thumbed through the pages. "Nothing," he said. He showed Roy a page penciled with figures. "You're paid up for a while yet." He dumped the record book and tossed Roy a rolled and banded newspaper. "Pretty soon, a new guy will be collecting."

Back on the porch, Roy was reading the paper aloud when Mrs. Kenny stepped from her front door. She was in her eighties and lived in the other half of Roy's double.

"Are you reading news to the dog?" she said. She pushed her aluminum walker in front of her and took a while to make it to the sofa. "I'm sick with the heat."

Roy said, "It's awful. I'm dripping on the funnies."

They sat for a while without speaking.

"I believe it's hotter out here," Mrs. Kenny said.

"It could be," Roy said. "You know, it gets a lot hotter than this in Greece. It gets so hot that at midday they just close everything. No one does a thing."

"Well, this is hot enough," Mrs. Kenny said. "What does that say?" She put a hooked finger on the column Roy was reading.

"It's Mickey Rooney," Roy said. "He's in town with a show. He says you've got to have your heart in it. Every minute." Roy roughed the fur on the red dog's neck. "The dog knows," he said.

"I guess so," Mrs. Kenny said. She was looking at the newspaper in Roy's hand. The hand and the paper were trembling.

"What's wrong with you?" she said.

"I'm having trouble," Roy said, "with sleep."

"Well, you listen to the music all night. You always play that radio."

"That's it," Roy said.

"You don't try to sleep. You listen to that music."

"Oh," Roy said, "that's probably it. I don't try."

STAY

WITH ME

GET OUT of my yard," Neal said. He was standing in his living room, between the pastel drapes at the picture window.

"Who are you saying that to?" said Neal's wife, Nancy.

"One of the Langhams. A girl."

"Sharon?" Nancy said. "Cindy?"

"This kid is getting a figure. The one with the majorette's baton all the time."

"Cindy."

"I hate her," Neal said.

Nancy said, "Get away from the window."

Neal looked at his feet, at the pearl-gray carpet under his loafers. "Quit telling me where to be," he said to Nancy.

"Then behave," Nancy said.

"Get out of the yard," Neal said to the window glass.

"Neal," Nancy said sharply. "Come on, Neal." She was frowning and pasting trading stamps into a paper booklet. She was sitting on the stuffed couch.

"In ten years of marriage," Neal said, "the best thing that's happened to you is being able to tell me to behave. You are delighted to be able to tell me to behave."

"Come on, Neal, I mean it," Nancy said.

Neal switched his gaze back to the window. "That's right," he said. "Walk all over my crocuses. Bat the heads off my roses with your baton. I can afford it. Here comes her sister to help her wreck up my garden."

"If she, or they, are really bothering our flowers, Neal, go to the door and politely tell them to stop."

"No, no," Neal said. "What the hell. Now they're clearing a little path for themselves to play in. That's right. Tread on those mums. The sister has a little scythe. Why don't they go get old man Langham to do it right with his Toro?"

"Is there anybody really out there, or are you just exercising your voice?"

"I'm just exercising my voice," Neal said. He went and sat beside Nancy on the couch.

"Settle down," Nancy said. She pushed a row of gummed orange stamps into the wet sponge that rested on the low table in front of her. "Settle down for Sunday," she said, and lined the row of stamps in the booklet and pressed them down with the heel of her hand. "Did you take a pill?"

"Honey, yes," Neal said.

There was something in his voice that caused Nancy to tip her head sideways and look at him. She made a noise with her mouth. "Neal?"

"Honey, I did. See?" He stuck out a flattened hand.

"See what?"

"I'm shaking. Are you happy?"

"I don't see any shake," Nancy said. She bent closer to Neal's hand and studied the long clean nails and thin hairless fingers.

"Great," Neal said. "Then my eyeballs are the things that are shaking. In my head."

"You're all right," Nancy said. "They wouldn't give you something —"

"We've had this conversation," Neal said. After a moment he said, "I am really shaking."

"Don't jiggle your knee," Nancy said. "Do something, why don't you?"

Neal got off the couch and dropped on his knee before the television. "I'll have a beer and watch a movie." He switched the channel knob around. "Two stations, and both of them have nothing but basketball."

"Turn it," Nancy said.

"We just get two stations. All that's on is this."

"You were going to fix the set," Nancy said.

"Well, there's nothing else on," Neal said. He sat back on the carpet and held onto the toes of his shoes. Ahead of him, the TV showed a player dribbling a basketball on the edge of the court, cornered by two members of the opposing team. People were clapping.

"Sunday," Neal said. He sighed and said, "If this wasn't Sunday, the Langham brats would be in school. Something else would be on television."

Nancy finished with her trading stamps and carried the swollen book into the kitchen.

"I'm making hot cocoa," she called to Neal.

"I'm going to have a beer."

"I'm making the cocoa for you, instead of a beer."

Whistles blew on the TV. A player was sent to the bench. The player held his clenched fists high over his head. Feet stamped. A large section of the crowd was put on the camera. Their fists were raised like the player's.

Nancy came back into the room, blowing steam from the top of a nubby ceramic mug. Neal was rocking on his bottom with his shoes in his hands.

"Pretty soon you can go back to work," Nancy said.

Neal squeezed his eyes shut and shivered like a wet dog. "Leebert Industries," he said. "Toledo Steel. Rafkin Bearings. Shipping and receiving. Thermocouplers. Mechanalysis. Mr. Hart and Mr. Fox. United Pap. United Parcel. The Telex machine." He began to make a weak, breathy laughing noise.

"I talked to Harry Hart," Nancy said, ignoring Neal's laughter. "You can't imagine how nice he was."

"I know he was," Neal said. He stopped rocking. "Tell me something new."

"You're not ashamed of seeing him, are you? He said the one thing he's most afraid of is you being ashamed to see him."

"He can rest at ease about that," Neal said. "Hart's a drunk, an embezzling crud, and so is his big buddy, Bill Fox."

"They've been fine to us," Nancy said. "Harry told me they're just chafing to see you get on with your life."

"Chafe away," Neal said. Then he said, "I like Harry Hart." He sighed and pushed in the TV control knob with the end of his shoe. The picture popped and the basketball game vanished. "Look," Neal said. "Us." He pointed to the TV screen, to his and Nancy's reflections. He lay back on the gray carpet and put his hands behind his head.

"In the meantime, there's a lot to do around here," Nancy told him. "You could get busy on the garage. Let's do fix the set. I'd like the slate put down for a patio before it starts to get really nice out."

"Ah, let me sleep," Neal said.

"I will not. The sun's still high. Do not go to sleep."

"Okay," Neal said.

"I'll perk coffee. You stay awake until ten or so, Neal. You haven't touched your cocoa."

"Why wait until ten, Nancy?"

She leaned forward on the sofa and clenched one hand. "You're sure feeling sorry for yourself today."

"Here we go," Neal said.

"What?"

"Why do you stay with me, Nancy?"

"I do wonder, Neal," she said.

"Big secret," he said. He sat up and spun his body around once on his bottom. He got to his feet and walked toward the door.

"Now where are you going?"

"No place."

"Good," Nancy said. "I'm going to start dinner pretty soon."

"I'll make my own," Neal said.

"No, Neal. We can't be doing things that way."

"Then don't dish the plates. I'll eat exactly what you eat, Nancy. Goodbye," he said. He snapped open the door, crossed through, and closed it behind him. He walked down his lawn, a short hill, and stopped under a sycamore tree.

Cindy Langham dashed past him and ran across the street to the yard of the house that fronted Neal's.

Neal sat on the curb. "You know what?" he said to the Langham girl. She was facing him from across the street, her eyes narrowed against the warmish early-spring sunlight. She had the baton yoked across her small shoulders and was resting both wrists on the shaft.

"What?" she said.

"If you come over here into my yard again, I'll have you arrested."

"I didn't come over to your yard. I was looking for our whiffle ball," she said. "Father said I could."

"Do you know what trespassing is?" Neal said.

The girl ignored him. She began to work her baton. Her long straight legs bent in a stationary march and her fine blond hair lifted, and she shook the hair down her back.

"Do you know what that word is?" Neal said. He stood up.

From the street, a large dog, an Irish setter, that was

leashed to a stubby retarded boy, broke away and bounded up to Cindy Langham. The dog fought with the girl for the baton.

"Blind him the way you did my cat," Neal said.

The girl was shrieking and laughing. "Come and get Lancer!" she yelled to the retarded boy, who was trotting toward her. The girl stepped away from the dog and used fingers to remove a banner of hair that had caught in her mouth. She held the baton high over her head. Without looking at Neal, she said to him, "I was never in your yard."

"If you say so," Neal said. He walked back up to his house and stood in front of it, between boxed shrubs. A window cranked open behind him.

"What are you doing?" Nancy said.

"The sun's getting ready to set," Neal said.

"It is not," she said. "You look ridiculous."

"Standing in my yard?"

"Shirttails out and staring off. No jacket."

"How do you know if I'm staring?" Neal said. "My back is to you. I don't need a jacket. It's late April. It's sunny. You could get a tan the way the sun is beating down." He squinted up at the sun.

"I have dinner ready," Nancy said.

"Fine. Eat it," Neal said.

"All right," Nancy said. "I'm calling Doctor Bruskin."

"Don't call Bruskin," Neal said.

"I don't know what else to do. I've been keeping a count on your pills, Neal. You've been skipping them. You skipped today."

"Would you like to shake all the time? Would you like that?" Neal said. "I'm not hurting anybody in my yard, standing here in the ruins of my roses."

"What am I supposed to do?" Nancy said.

"You figure that out for yourself. I'm just working on me right now."

"I want you to come in," she said. "I don't want to eat alone. I want somebody to talk to while I eat."

"Okay. Here I come," Neal said. "You should have just told me that in the first place."

FELT PIECES

THERE was dust in the air and in the light. Valery's chair stood in a shadow, away from the cone of sun coming through the window glass. She was reading from a library book in a Mylar jacket. But she could not concentrate. She read a sentence five or six times. "I saw the Earth cower." She read this again and again, and thought about the bad fit of her navy suit. The coat was biting beneath her arms. The skirt reached a little too far down her crossed calves.

"I saw the Earth . . ." Valery read, and with her free hand fluffed the short hairs over her ear.

Her daughter, Jane, was in the room, cutting pieces of felt, making a collage of a village to paste onto white posterboard. There were black avenues, a turquoise church, yellow houses.

The little girl wore clothes that Valery had made for her on their sewing machine. She wore a khaki jacket and a skirt of polished cotton. The jacket had dark shell buttons. The sewing had cost Valery a long weekend because the sewing machine was old and had to be cranked by hand, pumped by foot.

Valery closed the book without marking her place. She drank from a short glass of whiskey.

Jane was on her knees, tucking the felt scraps under each other, trading the colors, making a pinwheel, dividing it, making a fan.

Valery's eyes closed. Somewhere on the street a radio was tuned to a Canadian station. She heard a French-spoken monologue, the news. She heard the bump of Jane's bare feet on the uncarpeted stairs.

The girl brought a brush from an upstairs room. She ran it over her mother's hair. Straightening, Valery took a mouthful of drink. The ice cubes in the whiskey glass had dissolved to dime-sized circles.

"Was I asleep? How long?" Valery said to Jane, who shrugged.

Merle, Valery's A.A. friend, patted the screen door and pushed through. She was holding a lemon pie. "Oh, Val," she said. "What are we doing?"

"You should go," Valery said to Merle.

"I know that," Merle said, and sat on the sofa in her raincoat. Her legs straddled Jane's collage. Merle held the pie in both hands.

Jane was on the floor again, brushing her own hair and going through the magazine for the picture she was copying for her collage.

"Janey," Valery said, "take Merle's pie carefully out to the kitchen. Carefully." When Jane was gone, Valery said, "For the first time in a month I feel tired."

"What are you reading?" Merle said.

Valery passed her the book. Merle held it the way she had held the lemon pie, on her thighs. She said, "So much is marked out."

"It's a library book," Valery said. "Somebody else did that."

Jane came back into the room. Valery rested the whiskey glass on her bottom teeth and watched her daughter do yoga positions. "Show Merle the Cobra," she said.

Jane lay on her stomach. She laced her fingers behind her back and raised herself from the floor.

"Cripes!" Merle said. "I can't bear to watch." She said to Valery, "She's wonderful in those clothes."

"I know," Valery said. "I had a daydream that I made her four more of those skirts. Four shades of blue."

"Who really did all this crossing out?" Merle said, looking back at the book. "Wasn't it you?"

"Yes, it was me," Valery said. "I was so distracted, I crossed out the sentences I understood. That's how bad off I was. You can see how many I didn't understand."

"Look," Merle said. "Can you believe it?" She nodded toward Jane. Jane was lying on her back, breathing quietly. Her eyes were shut and her lips parted.

The women sat for a while, Valery drinking and Merle smoking. "Hey," Merle said, "do you think Jane would mind if I helped with her picture?" She leaned forward and fingered the cloth cuttings.

"Have at it," Valery said.

Merle worked from her leaning position.

Valery removed her suit jacket and wadded it. She got onto the floor beside Jane and put half the coat under each of their heads.

"You be here awhile?" she asked Merle.

"Yes," Merle said. "Where have you got it?"

"Same cabinet as always," Valery said.

Merle went to the kitchen and came back with a glassful of Valery's whiskey. She drank and she stood in the living-room doorway and she looked at Jane and at Valery, who lay with her eyes open.

"I feel wonderful," Merle said.

A Note on the Type

The text of this book was set in Sabon, a typeface created by Jan Tschichold, the well-known German typographer. Introduced in 1967, Sabon is loosely patterned on the original designs of Claude Garamond (1510–1561).

Composed by Publishers Phototype Inc.,
Carlstadt, New Jersey
Printed and bound by
The Haddon Craftsmen, Inc., Scranton, Pennsylvania
Designed by Margaret M. Wagner